$\mathcal{V}$OICES OF THE $\mathcal{S}$OUTH

It Is Time, Lord

Fred Chappell

IT IS TIME, LORD

Louisiana State University Press

BATON ROUGE AND LONDON

LSU Press edition published 1996 by arrangement with the author
First published by Atheneum
Manufactured in the United States of America
05 04 03 02 01 00 99 98 97 96   5 4 3 2 1

Library of Congress Cataloging-in-Publication Data
Chappell, Fred, 1936–
    It is time, Lord / Fred Chappell.
        p.   cm. – (Voices of the South)
    ISBN 0-8071-2119-3
    I. Title.   II. Series.
PS3553.H298I2   1996
813'.54–dc20   96-19218
                                                               CIP

The paper in this book meets the guidelines for permanence and dura-
bility of the Committee on Production Guidelines for Book Longevity
of the Council on Library Resources.♾

DEDICATED TO *Dr. William Blackburn*

AND TO *Bob Mirandon*

AND TO THE MEMORY OF *William G. Owens*

*Nam minima commoda non minimo sectantis
descrimine similes aiebat esse aureo hamo piscantibus,
cuius abrutidamnum nulla captura pensari posset.*

It Is Time, Lord

1

I WAS BORN May 23, 1931, in the house of my grandmother. No doctor could be found to attend, only a midwife from three miles away in the country. My birth was loud and troublesome; the midwife, who was but a young girl, fainted away and my father, who was assisting, had to force her again to consciousness. I lived in the room later for a long while with my grandmother. It was in this room that we took our meals and every night kept a watch until midnight, she reading the Bible, I myself reading a queer story of adventure. On the mantel above the iron stove there was a large clock, which was wound with a key stuck in two holes in its face. A brass pendulum swung inside the glass front, uttering a solidly satisfying click at each foot of its arc. My mother in the labor cried for the clicking to stop. My father opened the face and clutched the pendulum, but his hands so shook that he succeeded only in making the clicking faster. He was forced to take up a pair of scissors and a pencil and hold them on each side of the pendulum in order to halt its motion.

I was born in Gemini, which is the sign of the arms and denotes balance. We born in Gemini are fond of mathematics and science, or, perhaps, acting and oratory. We have a middling talent for commerce, are of a saving disposition, are moderate in all things. In short a fine sense of balance marks our undertakings.—Not so my sister, who is four years my junior. She was born in Leo, August 2, and they born in the sign of the heart have lofty minds and moral seriousness, dignity and firm will. Ptolemy of Pelusa hazards that one of the sign of the heart will achieve positions of honor and trust: thus, my sister has two children, and they are obedient. She never bends to them, and merely laughs at their egotistical whimsies.—She and I are temperamentally opposite. She is confident and graceful in her certainty that she always has the right in things, while I attribute my indecisiveness to my habit of weighing all particles of a problem. My two children obey me but tolerably, for I take their reasons seriously. The world my children see is very different from the world I see, but I discover in it a substance, and it is not less broad than my world. Leo, too, is a masculine sign, dry and barren, a fire sign; and so my sister has really the soul of a man, perhaps the soul of a prince. Gemini is also a masculine sign, but it is an air sign. An air sign has the disadvantage of inconstancy, as of the winds, but air is the temple of space, of infinity. Nothing so pours through me as the blueness of the sky in a cold, clear day; no eyes trouble me so much as the peculiarly flat blue eyes of babies or of ruthless blond women.

That room in which I was born had blue walls, too. They were plaster walls with tiny pimples everywhere, like a coat painted on. The ceiling was fairly high—it was rather an old house—and the single illumination was from a bulb suspended by a gilt chain from the center of the ceiling. When I was very young I liked to mount a chair and bat the bulb with a newspaper in order to watch the shadows of the furniture stagger on the floor, dart in and out beneath each object like animals frightened and bold by turns. The room always smelled of camphor, oil of wintergreen, and tonic: medicines my grandmother absorbed continually for her

4

varied complaints.

The house was brick and there were fourteen other rooms. It was set on a hill in the center of the farm. Three barns stood together two hundred yards east of the house; behind them pasture stretched over a hundred acres of hills, below them lay the grain and tobacco fields, and a crooked creek, gradually chewing away the edges, the course being twisted and spring floods coming annually. The stream was well populated with muskrats, too, and their burrows ran sometimes into the middle of fields. The bottom fields were the best evidence of the present fortune of the farm: my grandparents could neither afford to have the creek straightened nor to leave it crooked. The buildings were all in good condition and the land well cared for, but the fence rows were grown with ragweed and locust and sassafras bushes, a sign that tenantry was unwillingly employed.

The fourteen other rooms of the house I remember as being always cold and dark. My grandmother was unwilling to give a room heat or light except when it was absolutely necessary. When I was older I lived in an upstairs room with two gable windows facing west. The room was paneled with notched pine slatting, and in the stream of the grain I would find rivers with islands, flames, tongues, heads of dogs, men, and bears. A long ridge fenced away the town from the farm and when I darkened my room for the night the gray aureole of the town lights lay along the top.

But I did not live in this room until I was fifteen, when I had already felt the first vague desires of sexual life: to sleep all night in a muddy ditch, to hang dead by the toes like Mussolini, to eat hashish—I fancied that one ate it from a bowl with a spoon, that it was of the consistency of jelly and black and bitter. And too

5

—unfortunately—these upstairs bedrooms were furnished with dressing tables with large mirrors. For the vulgar saying that one cannot live on love is true only of romantic love, and certain persons there are who can live fatly on self-love, can devour themselves to the last gut and toenail, Narcissuses who play with themselves the game of Zeus and Selene.

And this is not on my part self-castigation for adolescent guilt. The chances are good that the remembrance is false. Pray God that it is. For the rich money of dream is generally debased by the counterfeiting of memory, and in the same manner certain reminiscences gain especial value by the significance of subsequent events. To illustrate, if a stranger approached you with a handful of diamonds, you would not attempt to judge his character by admiring his jewels. We can form no idea of the history or mind of a past century by reading its best poems, nor can we discover ourselves by the single remembrances that fasten to us.

I choose a single memory which has gathered such patina of usage that it seems much further distant than it is. My sister was three years old and she was following me to the barn. It was very cold. When the wind blew it hurt, but there was not very much wind. It hurt too when I walked fast, the cold air cutting my lungs as I breathed more deeply, and so I walked slowly.

Step for step behind, my sister whimpered. She wore only a little dress with puffy sleeves smothered in a thin blue sweater. She had long blond curls and I thought they were brittle because it was so cold and that they might splinter on her shoulders like golden icicles. It was late dusk and the moon was yellow, bulgy and low over the hills of the pasture, a soft handful of butter.

There were men in the barn I had never seen. They sat on sacks of crushed corn and cottonseed meal in the

6

dimness. They looked mute and solid. Someone said, "That's a little girl behind him."

One of the men rose and approached slowly. He was tall and his gray eyes came toward me in the dusk. His hair was blond, but not as yellow as my sister's. "Where you from, boy?" he asked.

"Home."

"Is that your sister?"

"Yes. She's Julia. My name is James."

"Don't she have something more than that to wear?"

"I told her not to come out with me."

"You better strike out," he said. "She'll freeze to death out here."

"Strike out?"

"You better light out for home." He rubbed his big wrists. "Hurry up and go on before she freezes to death."

"Come on," I told her. She was still whimpering. Her hands were scarlet, smaller and fatter than mine. I touched her hand with my finger and it felt like paper. There were small tears in her eyes, but her face was scared, not crying.

I started back. The rocks in the road were cold. Once I didn't hear her whimpering and I looked and she was sitting in the road. I went to her and took her elbows and made her stand up. "Come on," I said reproachfully, "you'll freeze to death."

We went on, but then she saw a great log beside the road, and went to it and sat. She had stopped whimpering, but her eyes had become larger. They seemed as large as eggs. "Please, come on," I said. "You'll freeze to death out here."

She looked up at me. I pulled at her. Her wrists felt glassy under my fingers. "What are you doing?" I cried. "Why won't you come on? You'll freeze to death." I couldn't move her. It terrified me because I thought

7

she had frozen to the log.

It had got much darker and the moon was larger.

I jerked her again and again, but she didn't get up. Nothing moved in her face. Two small tears were yet at the corner of each eye. She looked queer, stonelike, under the moonlight, and I thought something terrible had happened to her.

"What are you doing to her? Why don't you leave her alone?"

My father suddenly appeared behind me, huge and black in the moonlight. He too had a small tear in each eye. He was breathing heavily in a big jacket. White plumes of breath bannered in the air.

"What makes you hurt her? What gets into you?"

She raised her arms, and he gathered her to his jacket, holding her in both his arms as in a nest. She knotted herself against his chest, curling spontaneously.

He turned his back toward the moon and strode. Sometimes I had to trot to keep up, and I continued in the limplike pace until we got home.

"Open the door," my father said hoarsely. He knocked the door with his foot.

My mother stood waiting inside and looked through my head at my sister, red in my father's arms. "What happened?" she asked. Her mouth thinned.

I went to the brown stove and put my hand flat against its side, and it seemed a long time before its heat burned me. My face began to tickle.

"What were they doing?"

I walked to the window and looked at the moon huge and yellow behind the skinny maple branches. A dim spot emerged from the window pane as I breathed, and as I stood there it got larger and larger, like a gray flower unfolding, until it obscured the total moon.

This was winter, specifically January; spring is another matter entirely. April is even now chartreuse for me, a color which retains the dizziness and inspiring sickness of the liqueur. The new grass of April is chartreuse, and the new leaves on the long withes of weeping willows. It seems my father kept an ape, a tall, ginger-colored beast which wore a red collar about its neck, but was otherwise entirely free. The nameplate on the collar read: Modred. He had given me a long reap hook and told me to cut the lawn. The pale new grass was very short and limp. The hook would not cut it; the grass-blades bent under it, and seemed to squirm away from it. Finally I threw the tool down in exasperation. My father came out upon the porch with the ape —he was quite as horrid as Poe's ape of the Rue Morgue—and said to it, "You'd better get him before he gets any worse." The ape felt the back of its neck under the collar and put some lice in its mouth. Then it came down into the yard for me. I ran to a willow tree and climbed to the shuddering top before stopping, but when I looked down I looked into the face of the ape directly beneath me. It seized me by the ankles and pulled me down against its chest. I could hardly breathe. It clutched my left arm and bit away my hand. I could see the bare silver bones of my wrist. The ape looked down, and my father, who was standing at the foot of the tree, tossed it a salt shaker. It began to sprinkle salt upon my wrist.

So this is probably a dream, though perhaps it is injured by things which have since occurred or by dreams I have since received. But it is more tangible than many things encountered in the flesh. For instance, among our linens now is a washcloth with the print of a rose; nothing is more unreal than to see it floating alone, half-submerged, in the white bathwater. Or I would play chess or Chinese checkers with my grandfather and suddenly there would appear upon the squares of the board the hump and tail of Ursa Minor or the long spine of Draco. What is less real than this? We played on a marble chessboard which my grandfather had himself set in a heavy oak table he had made. To see these constellations emerge from the aggregate of pawns and knights was like seeing Atlantis raise its head out of the cold ocean, or, perhaps, like seeing in the marigold faces of human men the sudden roses of divinity: Dionysus before Acetes; Christ:

> *Lo, how a rose e'er blooming*
> *From tender stem hath sprung!*

My grandfather and I would befuddle the eternal summer afternoons with games: chess, checkers, poker. He sat in a leather rocking chair on the open porch. By him a small table held a pitcher of water, a glass, a pint of whiskey. He drank slowly and thoughtfully. Flies strutted on his knuckles. He had a very bald head, deep green eyes, the face of Sibelius with the identical veins distent on the temples. It was a face such as the Emperor Augustus must have had: and this was how he sat, the melancholy emperor of the afternoon. He was a builder of houses and a good carpenter, but now for nearly forty years he had been able to walk only with the support of a crutch and a cane. Sometime in his twenties his legs had been completely shattered in a sawmill accident, and, because medicine in that time and place had been so very bad, he had never recovered. In the afternoons he did not like to walk. Besides games his other amusement was swatting flies. He wore out any number of fly swatters before he fashioned himself a leather one from the tongue of an old shoe. Like my sister, he was born in Leo.

10

Leo is summer, a lion with a hide of shaggy gold. Its haunches are sunlight, its flesh the logos of God.

> *Strong is the lion: like a coal*
> *His eyeball, a bastion's mole*
> *His chest against the foe.*

My grandfather and my sister are searched into by this majesty, kneaded in the glory of it. But are we merely masks of the stars and seasons? Apple trees are of summer, too, but they remain in winter, and not entirely asleep. For my grandfather lived through many winters and died in a summer. Once, I remember, he and I walked together in a December morning. We walked through the orchard in the first heavy frost of the season—or at least it now seems that it was the first heavy frost. Suddenly he said, "Look out, boy. Reach me that apple." Above my head hung a great yellow apple, which somehow had escaped apple picking and autumn. I leaped as high as I could and felt it thud heavily in my hand. I gave it to him, and he, resting lopsided on his crutch, inserted both thumbs in the blossom end and tore the fruit into irregular halves. The meat was white as linen. The sunlight glittered on the moist flesh as on dew. Two black seeds glared from its heart. It was so cold it hurt my teeth.

Leo endures. There is summer in winter. My grandfather spent most of the winter before the cast-iron stove in the warm blue room. The stove was wood-burning; the top slipped sidewise on a socket hinge and chunks of wood were thrust in. Ashes and coals fell into a long, narrow trough beneath the grates. I used to lie on my belly on the floor and gaze through a small window into this trough. Everything grew small and the dropped cinders were great boulders and mountains. The scene was illuminated by the red-orange glare of the fire above. It was as arid as sand, and live coals dropped through the grates, splashing the walls with sparks. This is the best notion of hell. When I would dream or daydream of going to hell I always wound up in the bottom of that stove.

"Don't look into the fire so long, boy," he said.

"Why not?"

"It's bad for your eyes."

"How come?"

"You'll go blind if you keep that up long enough."

"Is it bad to be blind?"

"You can't see nothin when you're blind. Man that's blind is in bad shape. I used to know a feller in Fletcher Forks that was blind. He was sworped across the eyes with a sharp chestnut limb when they felled the tree."

"What did he do?"

"Well, he used to log a little. Had a good matched team, used to bring hardwood about halfway down Turkey Knob and J-hook it off the mountain."

"What's J-hook?"

"Look here." He held out his left arm, his hand bent toward the inside. His fingernails looked tough and oily, like a cow horn. "This here's your hook, and this here's your bar." He put his right forearm against his left elbow to show me. Then he picked up his crutch from the floor. "Now, this is the log, and your J-hook goes like this and the bar this way." He held the handle of the crutch in his half-open hand and laid his arm on one of the stocks. "You start goin down with your mules pullin the log, but pretty soon the log gets to goin faster and faster down the mountain. See how it goes? It's heavier than your mules are, put together. Pretty soon it's goin faster than your mules can trot, but see, you've already got you a chute built on top of some cleft that's handy to where you're haulin out, so you run on into the chute and kick your bar. When you do that it flips your hook out and the log's free from your riggin. The log slides down to the foot of the holler."

"What did the man do after he was blind?"

"Well, he couldn't do nothin much. He sort of got along doin a little cobblin, although he was never any great account at it. He couldn't make no shoes nor boots nor nothin; he could just fix em when they was tore up or wore out in the soles."

"If you can't cobble, what can you do when you're blind?"

"What I was goin to tell you about this feller bein blind was he was a chinchy sort of eater. He was about like you like that, I reckon. When I worked with him, he used to take me in home to eat with him. He ate out of a wood plate he'd made for hisself. He'd cut out little dips in it for all the kinds of food. He couldn't stand for his food to get all run together when he was eatin. He just wanted to eat one bite of one thing at a time and he figured out what he wanted to eat before-time and if he didn't want to eat one certain thing right then he'd wait till he did. He was the same way after he got blind, too, but he couldn't tell nothin about what he was doin. He'd say, 'Sary, what's this I've got?' And she'd say, 'That's beans, John.' In a minute he'd say, 'What's this, Sary?' She'd say, 'That's grits.' In a minute, he'd say, 'God gast it, Sary, where's the applesauce?' "

He threw back his head and laughed loudly. The walls seemed to creak with the laugh. His nose was bushy with black hairs and his cheeks had blue-red veins.

This was the summer which was in winter, but winter itself was never nearly so warm or humane. It was ominous and icy, like the first sentence of Wells's novel:

No one would have believed in the last years of the nineteenth century that this world was being watched keenly and closely by intelligences greater than man's and yet as mortal as his own, that as men busied themselves about their various concerns they were scrutinized and studied, perhaps almost as narrowly as a man with a microscope might scrutinize the transient creatures that swarm and multiply in a drop of water.

All the days were overcast or brightly cold. At night the stars shone like frost on steel. Everything seemed constricted in winter, locked. The cold allowed me little freedom of movement; it wasn't pleasant to stray too long from the stove. Ice sealed the puddles in the road, and the new ice which in the early morning had begun to form in the milk cans looked like broken panes of glass. I hated to leave the room at night to mount the dark stairs, to undress and lie in the freezing sheets.

Curiously, in winter I was not nostalgic for summer but for fall. As I feverishly shelled corn for the chickens, I would look at the great heaps of corn about me in the crib, remembering when we had gathered it. Most of it came from the field across the winding creek. It was gathered into the wagon drawn by the patient team. But before the wagon came it was pulled from the stalk and thrown into small piles, aligned as nearly straight as we could manage. Then the wagon came, knocking awry the stiff, dead stalks—I thought of chessmen swept from the board—and the corn was thrown in, and the wagon went creaking to the barn. We rode back. The horses paused at the edge of the

14

creek. Uncle George, who was the tenant and not really an uncle, shouted them in. "Whoo. Whoohaw. Goddamn you, get your feet wet here. I'll lay onto you proper. Whoohaw."

His son, Jarvis, rode beside him on the wagon seat. "What if old Miz Albert was to hear you talk like that in front of honeybunch?"

I lay behind on the piled corn.

"He aint hearin nothin to scare him, I guess."

The wagon squeaked and descended through the water. The water seemed darker now than in summer; it crawled and wavered around the wheels. Behind, on the sandy bank, were dark sliced wheel tracks.

This was the sort of thing I would remember in winter: coming from the fields itchy with beggar's lice and Spanish needles, or tired and dusty, but not hot, from the final urgencies of the hayfields. Blackbirds and starlings knotted the telephone wires; the mockingbirds had already gone, and the bluejays. For after supper there would be pie from new pumpkins, sweet and coarse and stringy.

After I had shelled the corn I would feed it to the chickens, imitating my grandmother in calling them: "Here, chickchickchick chickee. Here, chickchickchickchick chickee." They would come running and when a good number was gathered, I would toss the corn in bright handfuls, pretending that it was money I scattered. A red hen would pick up a grain, drop it, pick it up again, bite it, drop it, lose it to another red hen, peck her, be pecked fiercely in return, peck another hen, search for another grain of corn. Then I shucked corn for the horses and the mule and fed them shorts and brought them water. Then I tossed hay down into the lot feed rack for the cows.

The cows never looked to see whence their feed

15

came. They stuck their heads into the rack and the tossed hay fell over their horns and tangled on their broad brows. Occasionally they would shake it off. In the twilight they seemed warm and dim and eternal. If a lantern was lighted in the barn, it threw oblongs and blades of orange light into the lot.

The barns were on a hill, and I could stand in the road by them and see time itself stretching and breathing below in the bright days. In winter we pastured steers and yearlings in the bottom fields, where they grazed on the tough rye grass we had sown in midsummer. The cattle, "calves" they were called, all faced in the same direction, north-northwest, as they cropped in the mornings. About noon they all rested, lying among the broken cornstalks or on the bald spot where tobacco had grown. In the afternoon they began retracing their journey, grazing southeast toward the barns. Again, I was reminded of the black and red counters of the chess game. The steers in the fields were red-and-white or black-and-white. Or I could see the indeterminate masses of shadow laid down by clouds which flew slowly across the sky. In a flat country, the shadows of clouds upon the land are not seen: one is either in the shadow or on a level with it. But these cloud shadows are the best idea of time, for it is only islands of time which touch us, and the vehement deeps of time—think of an ocean or a wheatfield—are alien to us, even though we have floated them or sported within them from the time of our birth. Chambers Mountain, which stopped up like a cork the northern neck of the valley, gathered clouds about its high shoulders like mantles of state.

"Did you ever use to cobble for a living?" I asked him.

He turned his graven head upon me. The green eyes

16

rested, as if he saw me reborn. "I thought I told you once to get up off of your stomach."

"Yes sir."

"No."

"Don't you know how to, though?"

The stove was equipped with an iron footrail and he laid his swollen right foot upon it. "I've had to make my own shoes to do right since I was hurt," he said. "I can do a little. I always knock down the tacks in your shoes when they cut your heels, don't I?"

"Yes." I thought of the queer iron foot in the milkhouse. It was about three feet high, and, set in a block of wood, it pointed toward the sky. The foot was flat and really was only an iron sole, neither right nor left. When my grandfather worked on a shoe, he fitted it over this iron foot and hammered it. A shoe tack looked small, smaller than the hour hand of a wrist watch, in his great hand. His fingers were square and hard; they seemed mostly bone.

On the mantel above the stove the pendulum clock clicked. On both sides of it sat mayonnaise jars full of pencil stubs, broken fountain pens which were used as dip pens, glass gimcracks full of bank statements, i.o.u.'s, financial notes, and there were Bible commentaries and two or three odd volumes of an encyclopedia. I had once begun to read one of these volumes; I read about the aardvark, the aardwolf, and the Aarn River, and then I stopped. I knew all about Aarn from my grandmother.

She would sit under the single bulb reading the Bible. She rocked in a small rocking chair and flat globules of light rose and set like miniature moons in her spectacles. She licked her noded thumb when she turned pages.

"Son," she would ask, "the dogs licked the blood of

what great king?"

"Ahab," I answered.

"Ahab, did you say?" my grandfather asked. His voice said, I don't believe you.

"No . . . McNabb," said the redhaired man. "Charles."

"I thought I must not of heard right. Ahab was a Bible king."

The redhaired man nodded quickly. He seemed in a great hurry. He had blue eyes, as flat as glass, the color of oceans on maps. The hair began so suddenly and tightly on his forehead it seemed like a wig. He was smoking a cigarette. He stood just over the threshold of the warm room and seemed to want to enter. "You say you don't mind my using your phone?" he asked.

"How about the woman with you?" my grandfather asked. "Has she got a coat or somethin heavy on?"

"She's got a coat," he said. "How did you know she was with me?"

"I know your tracks," said my grandfather. "Or somebody's like yours. They're behind the big barn. That's where you pull your car in."

The man stared at him. "What's wrong?" he asked.

"No, I don't want you to call anybody on the telephone. I don't want nobody comin to fix your car with a no-count woman in it behind my barn."

"Wait a minute. I didn't know you objected to my parking there or I wouldn't have done it."

"You couldn't of asked me to let you, either. Not for lettin you lollygag with the town whores. Trouble is, I've found burnt-out cigarettes not more'n a foot away from the hay, where you've throwed em out. That barn would go up like gunpowder."

"You mean to tell me you really won't have the decency just to let me borrow your phone?" He seemed unbelieving.

18

. . . L'empereur a l'oeuil mort.

"I'll tell you 'decent,' " my grandfather said. "I don't see no decent feller around here. You can walk for a telephone."

"It must be two miles, at least."

"That ain't far for a young feller."

"Wait a minute . . ."

"Don't tell me to wait. You're a ragged-ass son of a bitch."

He slammed the door. It was as if he had been snuffed out like a candle flame. We listened to his hard footsteps, and then the outer door closed. The fire in the stove hummed. Outside, the November wind blew.

"I never did like a redheaded feller," my grandfather said.

When I answered her questions about the Bible correctly, my grandmother would smile and nod to herself in approval. "That's right," she said. "Now, can you tell who Abishag was?"

"No. I don't know."

Then she would tell me—but not just who Abishag was. She told the whole story of King David from the beginning. When she got to her question, she would stop and say, "Now *that's* who Abishag was." Then she would tell the story to the end, down to Absalom and his long yellow hair.

These nights seemed eternal. Nothing moved in the room but the hand on the pendulum of the clock until my grandfather decided he wanted water. He rose painfully out of his chair and went to the kitchen. The sound was: *bup, swiss, thum:* first his cane forward, then his right foot dragged across the worn linoleum, then his crutch and left foot forward together. His hands were bald and white as metal on the sticks.

The fire in the stove hummed and belched.

In the kitchen, the water waited in a chipped porcelain pail in the sink. The rectangle of the window, patched with a black angle of the roof and a few stars or the moon, floated on the water like a piece of cheesecloth. But, when I bent over it to pull the dipper up, a great black head rose from the bottom of the pail. Disturbing the dipper made the whole fabric quake and waver. I thought of how a pattern in the slatted pine paneling of my bedroom would change from the head of a snake to the head of a bear to a pathetic ghost. I would shiver because it was very cold. I could not understand how everything changed and yet was always the same in the end.

"It bucks me up," said my grandfather in a July. "But it's just for old men like me; it ain't for young fellers."

"Maybe it will buck me up, too," I said. I wanted some of the whiskey he drank during the chess game.

"I've told you no," he said, "and you know better than to keep whinin. When I know you're old enough, I'll give you some."

"When will I be old enough?"

"When I've decided you are."

"How does it buck you up?"

"Changes a feller's outlook a little. Changes things, swaps em around a little better."

"I don't see anything changed."

"You don't know what to look for, yet, do you?"

"I don't see how it changes and don't change at the same time."

"Well, that's one of the things you don't know. Check."

His knight and rook menaced my king. I moved the wrong pawn.

"Keep your eyes open, boy," he said. "Watch what you're about."

20

"Are you goin to buy me that Canadian Mountie suit?"

"What do you want to look like your pants are full of corncobs for?"

But the patterns in the pine wall changed and the wall didn't change. And shadows changed, but the objects which created the shadows didn't change.

In a December my grandmother asked me not to bat that light bulb with a folded newspaper. "It makes it hard for me to see the words," she said, licking her knotty thumb.

"Yes mam," I said.

The bulb still swung slowly. I had been watching the shadow of the hanging edge of a tablecloth. It ran on the floor in and out from beneath the table, and it was shaped like a small black rat. I watched the straight shadow of a chair seat go back and forth like a windshield wiper. I looked under the door to watch the bar of shadow squeezed down by the swaying light. There was no shadow beneath the door. There was a pink glow as thick as a finger. I watched it a long time, and my eyes began to ache.

"What was that last chunk you put in the stove?" my grandfather asked. "It don't smell right, someway."

"It was just green red oak," I said. I could smell nothing but the medicines which always odored the room. I rubbed my eyes. The pink bar under the door had turned orange.

My grandmother had stopped reading. Both she and my grandfather sat silent.

I went to the door. "I don't know why this door's so hot," I said. The knob was slippery in my hand.

"Don't you open that door. You get everybody's coats out of that closet. Hurry up." He held both his walking sticks in one hand, and raised himself very suddenly. "Mamaw," he said, "put the papers on the mantel in my coat pocket." He hobbled to the telephone. "Come here," he told me, "and call this here number." He pointed to a number penciled on the wall.

My arms were full of coats. "The house is on fire," I said.

"Hurry up," he said.

Outside, a dry snow covered the ground. The trees looked pink, and it was very cold. We walked only about a hundred yards. Through the windows, the flames looked like fine ladies and gentlemen dancing at a great ball. I had never seen so much light. Chambers Mountain blotted out the last star in the Big Dipper, and, as I watched, light suddenly filled the windows of the tenant house.

There were silent tears on my grandmother's cheek, and a knot pulsed in my grandfather's jaw. "Them red-headed fellers is all no-count," he said.

"I'm going to kill that son of a bitch," I said. I was nine years old.

2

MY GRANDMOTHER was very tall, taller than my grandfather, who had been bent by stooping to his walking sticks. She was five feet eleven inches. She was as straight and firm as the edge of a door, and her carriage was perfectly balanced and easy. Tall as she was, she was yet graceful. Her shoulders were wide and her body of a middling slender build, so that her dresses—which she generally fashioned for herself—fell in straight lines from her shoulders. These dresses were all of solid colors: dark green and dark blue predominated among them. She was never without an apron, and in the deep pocket of this garment carried string, a paring knife, some spools of thread with a needle, a thimble, apple peelings, perhaps, a pencil stub grimy with use, a scrap or two of paper, and mail. She carried a handbag only when going to church or to market. These aprons were almost always entirely plain, the edges hemmed merely, and only occasionally had she sewn on red or yellow bias binding. Her dresses, too, were always very severely cut, though she would sometimes allow large pleats under the shoulders so that the cloth fell in large folds, heightening my impression of her dresses as judicial gowns or choir robes. She wore thick cotton hose, the color of creamed coffee. Her shoes were always black, the toes squared away, the leather decorated with perforated swirls. Going to market or to church she wore black store-bought dresses, throwing a light silver- or gold-threaded shawl over her shoulders. These were long shawls; the tasseled fringes brushed her wrist as she walked. Her hats too were black, with frowsy little dotted veils which covered none of the face. Working at home or in the fields she wore the kind of sunbonnet you find in the hillbilly comic strips.

I remember that her hair was first the vague gray of a cobweb or a glass curtain, and that it later turned stark white like bone china. Her forehead was high; her complexion good, though neither entirely fair nor entirely dark. Her face was wrinkled, especially about the eyes. Her cheeks were wrinkled, but not about her high cheekbones, where the flesh was firm and the color still pink. Her eyes were brown, with flecks of a darker brown; they were not striking eyes. She always wore bifocals with tiny, very delicate gold rims. Her teeth were of course not natural; I used often to find them lying on the window sill over the kitchen sink. Here she scrubbed them with salt or baking soda. Lying out, they seemed frightening, a dead animal. Her mouth was firm, her lips somewhat thin; her upper lip was short and slightly downy, like the lip of the princess in *War and Peace*. Her chin was round and smooth, her jaw line strong and straight.

Her wrists were large, the tarsal bones enlarged and prominent. The veins were enlarged, too. They were blue, very noticeable. On her hands, the skin was dry and weathered. When she twisted her hand, each pore made a tiny wrinkle, and when I touched her wrist it seemed as hard and bare as furniture. Her hands were knobby and calloused and she had great ugly knuckles. The fingernails were short, broad, square, with minuscule ridges. The fingernail of her left second finger was black and curled inward from some former accident.

24

When her hands were cold she would hold one in the other, like a ball. And when they were wet, she would dry them by rubbing them once on the apron, flat against her thighs. This is how a man dries his hands.

She had large bones, and her frame was large. Like Sherlock Holmes, she had strength without apparent muscularity. I have often thought that her tendons and ligaments must have been extremely powerful. Her fingers, which seemed clumsy and forgetting, adapted themselves to any tool, pitchfork or paring knife. She peeled an apple by putting her thumb on the base of the sharp edge, with the dull edge against her knuckles, and the handle resting lightly in her palm. She whittled the peeling away, stroking toward her body. The chips of peeling fell in her aproned lap.

With her Sunday dresses she wore rather large brooches of intricate design, made of brass and green glass. Lying on her dressing table, they looked like exotic insects. Also on her dressing table were a brush, a comb, a bottle of hair oil, a box of powder, a tinted picture of Franklin Roosevelt, wearing a deadly sincere expression. She was very likely to use too much face powder when she dressed, perhaps because she was careless, or maybe the mirror was too dark for her to see her reflection well. Grainy patches of powder often were on her cheeks and were noticeable when she smiled.

She had a very silent smile, which drew becomingly from the gravure of her face: it did not wrinkle her face the more, but hid advantageously among the other creases. When she grinned she hid her mouth with her dry hand. The gesture seemed immoderately coy, considering her age, but she hid a gap in her teeth: she had once dropped her dental plate in the sink. She never frowned, but instead drew the corners of her mouth down, elongating the short upper lip, until her mouth was a straight line. Like most elderly persons, her face exhibited little range of expression. When she read, she raised her eyebrows.

Her movements were as graceful as the nature of farmwork permits. Gentleness moved her body. She was wholly feminine, having been born on the last day of June in the sign of Cancer, a watery, fruitful, feminine sign. She had the virtues of women: keenness of mind, moral austerity, quickness and cleverness in business matters. Cancer is the sign of the breast, and the time of Cancer is a fruitful time for all things, even noxious growths. Her proper element was autumn, the harvest season, the rainy season.

She was then taller than I now am, for I stand only five feet eight inches. I weigh about one hundred fifty pounds, have gray eyes, muddy blond hair. My hair has slight waves which my parents nursed for me from infancy and which have begun now in my thirtieth year to straighten. My face is oval and fair and forgettable. My mouth is handsome in its way, but colorless; my eyes placid. My build is rather slight; the bones are small. My hands seem feminine, almost delicate: they are very white.

My disposition is not amiable, but, rather, amenable. I am willing for any interesting undertaking, but rarely enthusiastic. I rarely anger, but can withstand a great amount of vexation: in short, I am easily put upon. But I am not often treated so, for I am retiring, if not really shy. Like Hazlitt's Hamlet, I am more interested in my own thoughts than in the world around me, but

I am not Prince Hamlet, nor was meant to be—

I have no great personal problems, because my thoughts are only accidentally concerned with myself.

26

For me an abstract system is worth a hundred disparate data. I do not read the newspapers, I do not worry about money.

Even so, I am a very prudent person, and do not make decisions easily. To decide which necktie to wear is a source of the greatest confusion. I cannot make up my mind what I might like for dinner. I am introversive rather than extroversive, but I find myself *per se* uninteresting, and it seems that my self is but a key to some more important matter. Unfortunately, I am unacquainted with this other matter. What is paramount here is that I am by nature blind to a greater part of the world about; I am sealed away from the most of my life. This is an invaginate existence: much too dull to think about for its own value.

The things that interest me are faces, books, flowers, images, sports. I find no more durable pleasure than reading early Christian history, but I am excited by the imaginings of my children and the dreams of my wife and myself. I remain fascinated by my profession: I am a Methodist minister.

Among the questions one is asked before ordination in the ministry is: Do you expect to achieve perfection, with the grace of God? At least, this is the essence of the question; I have forgotten the exact words. One must answer, Yes. Again: Do you expect to achieve this perfection in your lifetime? Again: Yes. And, I have often wondered how seriously one is expected to take these two questions. In truth, I believe that perfection will work itself out—on the rare occasions when it is going to—despite anyone's efforts and quite regardless of the grace of God. It depends on where you stand to look at the time of your life.

For instance, I once attended the hospital deathbed of an old man who belonged to my congregation. He was a very old man, a farmer, a faithful church attendant. He had been involved in a highway accident. His hair was white and his face, too, was white, drained. He spoke slowly and thickly and regarded his imminent death calmly.

"Do you have a special burden you would like to pray to God to absolve you of?" I asked.

He was silent a long time. "Yes," he said finally.

"Would you like to tell me, or would you like to offer silent prayer?"

Long silence. "No . . . no," he said. "I can't pray. . . . I don't regret it . . ."

This is the kind of perfection that flowers despite God's grace; it is essentially the same perfection one feels in the first breathing of spring or the first spreading of a new linen tablecloth.

My grandmother lived to see me made a minister and to hear some few of my sermons, and this fulfilled perhaps her fondest hopes. My grandfather did not survive so long. I don't know how he would have felt about my profession. My memory vaguely hints that his attitude toward the ministry was equivocal, although his respect for the Bible was thorough and literal.

"You hear sayin now that the world's round like a orange," he once told me. "But it don't say nothin about it in the Bible, and the Bible mentions about everything else, I reckon: the radio, and television, and the airplane. But it don't say nothin about the world bein round."

"Do you think it's round?" I asked.

"Well, them science fellers generally know what they're talkin about, but I don't know. I passed a lot of flat country on my way to Oregon—miles and miles of it, farther'n I could see, but it didn't look round to me."

"Does the Bible say anything about whiskey?" I asked.

"It says, 'Do not look upon the wine when it is red.' "

"I'll take two," I said. He dealt me a five and a Jack of Diamonds. The Jack had blue eyes and a stiff yellow mustache.

"How will you open?" he asked.

"Three," I said. I laid three finishing nails in the center of the table. I sang,

> *"Jack of Diamonds, Jack of Diamonds,*
> *Jack of Diamonds, I cry,*
> *If I don't get rye whiskey,*
> *I'll live till I die."*

"Hold up," he said. "Who's been learnin you that?"

"Hurl," I said. Hurl was Uncle George's boy.

"What's he know about it?"

"I don't know."

Uncle George was about thirty-five years old, hardly old enough to be called "uncle" as a term of respect: it was merely a nickname. He was rather short, had sandy hair, gray eyes. He was as tough and warped as first-growth hickory. He usually wore overalls, a sweatshirt, and Army boots, for he had fought in the Second World War.

I remember once—I was older then—we were painting the barn roof. We were painting it a dull red, the color of a rank chicken. We bent over in the sun. A bursting sun filled the sky. *Pitch, pish:* amorphous areas of gray zinc, created like Asias, wobbly cats, things any-shape. I thought of the pine slatting in my old bedroom, before it had been rebuilt and painted white. Sweat dripped off our faces into the swathes of paint. I was dizzy from bending and from the odor of paint

and turpentine, and when I stood the emerald landscape oozed and wavered like steam from a kettle. It
was far down because the barn sat on the edge of a hill
on one side. Below, the fields, where I could watch the
shadows of clouds, lay squared or catty-cornered, green
candy in a box. To the north, the heavy blue-green tri-
angle of Chambers Mountain like a smoky ghost.

Uncle George said, "It's time for me to get some
air."

We went slowly to the corner of the roof and sat.
The tin burned my hams I had been working all sum-
mer, from the time school was out until now, dead
August, to buy shares on a car with a friend.

"Look at that," said Uncle George. "My crazy old
hound's moving them pups again." The spotted dog
came out of the barn on the other side of the road. A
pup dangled blindly in her jaws. "I bet a pretty she
takes him back out to the house. She's moved them
pups eight times in the past two weeks. She had em in
that barn, and then she moved em down in the weeds
next to the cow lot, and then she moved em out to my
basement, and then she moved back out to this here
barn." The dog padded in the dusty road, headed for
Uncle's house.

I stuck my belly out. My back was tired from bending. I looked toward the tenant house where Uncle
lived. Two lines of washing winked in the sun. "Look,"
I said, "look how those sheets are flapping. But there's
not the first sign of a breeze up here."

"I know it," said Uncle. "Look how that tobacco's
yellowin up. Won't be long before I have to start cut-
tin it."

I knew I'd be in school by then. "I don't care," I said.
"While I'm sitting there taking my ease, I'll think about
you cutting that tobacco. And loading it, and hanging
it on those wobbly tier poles."

He spat over the edge of the roof. "It's all one to me," he said.

I laughed. "Yes, I'll think about you laying those heavy sticks on the wagon, and dragging them off, and climbing up under the roof with them."

"Don't worry, honey. Your time's comin."

"No sir," I said. "I can't see it. You won't ever catch me dirt farming. It doesn't get you anywhere. You can turn up these same rocky hills here for the next fifty years, and still never have money to stuff a sock full of nickels."

"It's a living."

"That's not what I'm looking for."

"It's plenty, though. By God, I was in Saint Lô, France, durin the war. They wasn't a leaf left on the trees. It was the middle of the summer, too. And you know what happened? Them Frenchmens had cooked em and eat em all up, in salats and things."

"That doesn't hurt my conscience," I said. "I'm not going to start a war. I just want to get me a good job somewhere, to make enough money to live decently."

Uncle shrugged.

"How are we going to paint the other side?" I asked. "It's too steep to stand on."

"That's why I brung the rope," said Uncle. "I reckon it'll just about fit you, while I stay up on the ridgepole and hang on. As long as I hold on, you aint got nothin to be worried about."

"I'm not worried."

The sun broke, an angry chrysanthemum molting. We painted a long while, and then he fixed the rope about my waist. We stood splay-footed on the apex.

"There goes them McNeal girls through the corn-field," said Uncle. "I wonder what they've lost in the cornpatch."

"Nothing they can find," I said. "They're going

down to splash their feet in the water. That's hot work, loafing around the house."

We watched the slow progress of the girls, the tall corn shaking as they threaded their way through it toward the creek. The summer shimmered.

"Here I go," I said. Taking up brush and bucket, I inched down the side. "I hope you've got a strong grip."

"You be careful there, boy." My grandfather stood in the road above the barn.

"Well," I said.

Uncle was looking back over his shoulder. "Here comes old Sheba with another pup," he said.

"You better keep your eyes peeled," said my grandfather. "The boy's in a dangerous place."

I looked up at Uncle. He had given the rope two turns about his waist, and twisted it over both forearms. "I'm all right," I said. "Don't worry about me."

I painted a long while, sweat soaking the back of my shirt. My wrists were shiny.

"Whoo," said Uncle, "naked as a jaybird!"

"Who?" I asked.

"Them McNeal girls have took off every stitch. They're dobblin about in the creek without a stitch."

When I stood up, I stepped in the patch I had just painted. I fell on the sticky tin, and rolled off the edge. The hard rope took away my breath. Back and forth beneath me the ground ebbed as I swung from the roof, and I could smell the weeds in the sun, and see in the grasses a glitter of mica or glass.

"Are you all right, honey?" asked Uncle.

"I told you to watch what you were about," said my grandfather.

"God damn it," I said, "goddamnit, you old hopping Jesus."

32

That night my mother went round and round me, painting with an alcohol-soaked patch of cotton at the broad raw red streak the rope had rubbed on my waist. The alcohol smelled fresh and cold, and the long smart of it felt refreshing. Short and slender—she was but a tiny woman—she did not have to bend far over to doctor me. Smiling placidly as she worked, she was poking gentle fun, the only kind she knew, at me.

"I would think a young man on the roof of a barn would remember to be careful," she said. "If I were high up in the air I believe I wouldn't have but one thing on my mind."

"It was just an accident," I said.

"If you found yourself a girl friend, some nice young lady, you wouldn't have accidents like that," she said. She passed her cool hand across the back of my head. "Curiosity doesn't always have to kill the cat." She stepped away from me and looked at me carefully, her head cocked to one side like a catbird. She looked merry, but not unnecessarily or unjustly so. She held the bottle of alcohol in one hand, the blob of cotton in the other.—I have often remembered her like that. I was old enough to think, If it wasn't for her and grandmother, the men in this family would have killed themselves off long ago.

"Does it burn much?" she asked.

"It hurts good," I said.

3

H I M S E L F, the Emperor Augustus, was born September 23, 63 B.C. This day is under the sign of Libra, the Scales, but Sextilis was the month of his greatest triumphs, and the Senate voted that Sextilis be renamed Augustus. And this was the month in which my grandfather was born. One of the favorite maxims of Augustus was: "He who goes a-fishing with a golden hook will catch nothing nearly so valuable as that which he chances." To this my grandfather would subscribe, and so must I, although I recognize that it is in a way sacrilegious. This ministry of the Gospel is not for the timorous.

But, on the other hand, prudence is its own reward, and it is for this heresy that I condemn myself. Let it be. I can face hell, I think, with more composure than I could face any single day of my past come back to accost me, through which I would have once more to survive. Nietzsche remarked that to want an instant of one's past returned is to want it all returned—not just the enjoyment of the moment, but also one's regrets and fears which are coexistent with this enjoyment— but even this does not state the whole case: for to wish a past instant returned is to wish for death. The past is an eternally current danger, in effect, a suicide. We desire the past, we call to it just as men who have fallen overboard an ocean liner call, because we must predict the future. But this prediction, which is most necessitous, we cannot achieve. We back into the future, and are blind to what happens until it has already occurred. Then we only see it receding, metamorphosing with distance and distorted with memory's impure Doppler effect. As far as event is concerned, the mind is an isolated citadel standing in a desert. Miles of sand surround it. A starry sky stretches overhead. The face of God never leans toward it, and in the desert nothing moves. The citadel itself is peopled only with thin ghosts.

An acquaintance once told me that he read a translation of the *Iliad* when he was about ten years old, and that his mother died when he was nine. He can remember Achilles better than he can remember his mother. He has never read the book since, and I am almost certain he is afraid to. This is the kind of thing the past is: it is not unchanging. It grows up soon with weeds and underbrush like a dangerous trail. It sours and rots like old meat in the mind. It is a huge sea with titanic currents—like any sea. And he who fishes it must use a golden hook, he must plunge himself as bait into its depths, and if his past does not devour and destroy him wholly, his luck is insuperable. The self is the golden hook which is too valuable to cast into former days; no line is strong enough to hold it to the present and to the hope of futurity once the cast is made. The self is very precious, too; it is only with the self, open-eyed and sober, that we can accept Christ and the salvation of God. I do not trust another; I do not trust a book, a rock, a stream; I do not trust my friendly Doppelganger who ranges my dreams and daydreams: these are all traitors, and they will murder me with the Judas kiss of the unconscious. Sleep, the night, belong to the unconscious, but one must take care to cut it off, like an electric light, at dawn. The day has no business with the belly of the mind. For when the mind dies, it goes belly up, a poisoned fish, the sickly white of the unconscious nakedly displayed.

Put it this way: you don't plow with a tiger; you don't hide your money in a furnace. Blake said, "The tigers of wrath are wiser than the horses of instruction," but if what he said is true, it is better that we remain stupid. One hears that he must be sensitive and empathic to the conditions of others. But one can be so sensitive that he is helpless, a mere pincushion, a professional victim. Mark the difference between pity and compassion. Do not love your neighbor as yourself; love him as your brother. One loves oneself too dangerously. Pity is hypochondria, narcissism, one must love men as one loves brothers: with the fine edge of a love, a razor dividing affections and hate.

Take yourself up.

. . . My sermon clanks shut.

4

HERE IS MY sister come to see—not to visit—me. We sit in what I for a joke call my "study," a room piled with books, newspapers, letters, the pulp magazines I have collected since I was a kid, dusty photographs. I never allow my wife to straighten up this room, or even clean it. I never clean it myself, and there are actually cobwebs in two corners of the ceiling. Sylvia, my wife, has brought coffee to my sister and me, taking, in the errand, care not to look at me. She does not look at me, and from this I am assured of what I had suspected: she has asked Julia to come to speak to me. Sylvia goes out to care for my sister's children and our own while Julia and I talk.

My sister digs in her square leather pocketbook for cigarettes. I hold the match for her.

"Well, James?"

"How's it going?" I ask.

"All right, I suppose. You know how it is." She leans back from the match, blowing smoke straight toward me. She is wearing a matching outfit, equivalent to a man's blue serge business suit. She is slim and always looks cool, like a new edition of the Bette Davis of the 1940's. If she were a man, she would make a good first lieutenant. "How are things with you and Sylvia?"

Not "you-all" or "you two," but "you and Sylvia."

"Fair enough, I suppose," I say. "What was it she wants you to tell me?"

To show very mild surprise, Julia has a habit of drawing her lower lip down, thinning her nose; a habit characteristic of men who wear stiff mustaches. This tic means that she has noted the dustiness and disorder of the study, and maybe, since she rarely turns her head toward the things she looks at, the cobwebs too. "The trouble is, I don't believe she knows herself, exactly. She doesn't know what you're up to since you left your job; she says you won't tell her. Or don't tell her."

"She's worried about money too, I guess."

"Well, if you have suddenly got rich it would ease her mind to know it." This is a sentence my father might have spoken.

"No."

"But still it's been three months now you haven't worked?"

"Yes."

"All she knows is you're here, usually in this room, or you're somewhere else."

"It wasn't that much of a job to begin with." I was production manager for Winton College Press. A small press, small salary, slight books.

"She hears you typing, but you tell her you're not writing a book."

"Sometimes I type some stuff, but I'm not writing anything. Look. You know I can't tell you anything I haven't told her. The fact is there's nothing to tell. As far as I know, there's nothing to tell."

Julia pulls the dustiest sheet off the table and reads aloud, "*I was born May 23, 1931, in the house of my grandmother. No doctor could be found to attend, only a midwife . . .*" She holds the sheet well away from her immaculate suit. "The story of your life?"

"No," I say. "The way that thing turns out, I'm a Methodist preacher."

38

Her laugh is not like her voice. She has a deep mannish voice, but her laughter is pitched high and sounds like a little girl's. "It's not your life, then," she says.

"I don't think so."

"Well, I should say not. When was the last time you were near a church?"

"I don't know. A long time ago."

"Why did you write that, then?"

"I don't know."

"Are you drinking now? I mean, much?"

"Some, not much."

"Well, I guess there really isn't anything to say," she says.

"Listen," I say, "why is it it seems to me that you're older than I am? I'm four years older than you. It used to be that I knew I was the older, but now it seems you're older."

"Well, there you've got me," she says, shrugging her straight shoulders. "Is it important to you?"

"I don't know that either," I say. "I don't even know how you find out what is important. Does it seem to you now that I'm younger than you are, or is it still the same as it used to be?"

"I hadn't thought about it." She appears to consider; that is, she does not think about it, but puts on the face of brief pondering. "It does seem that you seem younger than I used to think of you, but younger than I—that's a different thing." She picks up a paperbound novel from the clutter on my desk. *The First Men on the Moon.* Your reading habits haven't changed much." She puts it down, picks up *The Blue Atom.*

"Yes," I say. "They have, really. I never read anything now that I haven't read before." I see her peek at an open copy of a 1940 issue of *Doc Savage.*

39

She gives me a full, narrow stare. Her notion is that you can always learn about people by looking them straight in the eye. "Was it really so much better when you were younger?"

"No," I say. "It was much worse."

Later the same day when I am drinking a beer in a greasy bar, Preach tells me that he wishes he was back again in high school. "I never did get past the tenth grade," he says.

"What do you want in high school?" I ask.

"What I mean is, I wish I'd knew then what I know now." He gives me a black wink, and I wonder, Why does everyone make faces at me?

"What do you know?"

"I mean about the girls, man. I could have done good if I'd have just knew it." He leans back in the sticky plastic-covered booth. The yellow booth light spreads on his bony face. Thin, colorless lips; plaid sport coat, thin black tie; dirt around his collar; yellowish teeth. Rank, red, crisp hair pulled tightly to his head.

"Preacher, you're sure one son of a bitch," I say. I try to make it sound admiring, and I shake my head.

"I do all right," he admits. "I've done all right ever since my divorce."

"You really divorced?"

"Separated two years almost," he says. "Final any day now."

"Preach," I say, as if beginning the conversation again, "you haven't worked now for a year. You're on steady unemployment. What do you do all day?"

"I make the rounds," he says.

"What rounds?"

40

"You know, man. Here, there, and everywhere. Why, I'm all over hell and half of Georgia. You know how I am."

"You ever preach any?"

"I preach a hour a night whenever Orville Sadie brings his church revival in town."

"You're really a preacher, then."

He brings out his wallet: brown leather with a boots-and-saddle design stamped into both faces, leather laniard thong binding all the edges, the kind of wallet convicts make in prison to sell for cigarette money. He hands a white card to me. True Gospel Church of the Holy Light: photograph of a small brick building. An address in Gainesville, Florida. Preacher's name typed in the space: James D. Smathers, Jr. Back of the card blank. "That's my license," he says. "I was ordained through this correspondence course."

"What do you have to learn? All about the Bible and that sort of thing?"

"They tell you about the Bible," he says, "but you don't have to read but the main parts and read up the literature they send you. The main thing is, you have to believe and you have to know you believe."

"Believe what?"

"You have to believe in God's glory and the grace of Christ. Then you know everything's all right."

"I'd better get on back home," I say.

"What're you driving?" he asks.

"Just my Ford. What I always drive."

"I sure would admire to get over to Apex tonight," he says. "There's always something over there. I know a lot of people over there."

Apex is fifty miles. Light blue horizon in the west, the sun just gone down; darker in the east we head toward, and a dim piece of the moon up. Preach hands me one of the pints he insisted we buy before leaving Winton. Medium good bourbon, warm from the bottle, sweetish. He turns on the car radio.

"It doesn't work," I say.

"You ought to get it fixed," he says. "Easier when you have a good radio in the 'chine."

"What's easier?"

Another silly grimace. "Easier with the girls, man."

"Preach, you know I'm married. My wife's at home."

"What she don't know won't hurt her, will it?"

"Preach, listen, how old are you?"

"Twenty-nine. Why?"

"I just wondered." He too is younger than I, by two years. But I had thought he was older, although I couldn't have said how old. Yet not very long ago I would have said, if I had known him then, that I was older. It seems to me that I am younger than everyone I know. I don't know why I think about this older-younger idea.

Apex is a small hot, flat town, a pimple on the belly of North Carolina. Stoplights hung neatly at intersections, a pleasant moderate presence of green and pink neon. The familiar shops: a jeweler, a single bleak hotel, hamburger joints, a couple of billiards- and-beer halls. I begin to sweat. I cut the block around the hotel and head back the way we came.

"Where the damn hell are we goin?" Preacher asks.

"I've never been in this town," I say. "I've got to go back and come again."

"What the hell for?" When I don't answer, he gets the paper sack from the glove compartment and takes a longish pull. When he puts the bottle back into the compartment, one of John's toy firetrucks falls out. Preacher tosses it back in.

I turn around in the road, pulling onto the shoulder

on both sides. We go back. Apex, Bird Sanctuary. It is better this time. I'm more in control, and everything looks fresh and familiar. School kids going on a date to the one movie house, two waddling old maids; one young hood in a beer joint watches me speculatively. He had seen me the first time through.

"Where to?" I ask Preacher.

"I aint sure I know," he says. "Maybe we better go back and come again until I get the road learned."

"Twice is plenty."

"Hook a right the next red light, and then your second left."

It is a housing development, the houses as alike as pieces in a monopoly set, the lights in the houses like spots on a tablecloth.

"Here you go," says Preacher.

One like the others, but with the grass worn away on both sides of the cement walk, showing hard red clay. A rusty tricycle in the yard, turned on its side; other mostly broken toys scattered about. Every light in the house seems to be burning. I can hear the television set as soon as I get out of the car. Preach walks in without knocking; I follow hesitantly. One kid—I can't tell which sex—sits on a battered coffee table, tearing pages out of *True Confessions*. An older boy perched on a hassock about eighteen inches from the television screen. *Maverick* is loudly in evidence.

"What are you doing here, James Smathers? You know better than to come back here."

A fat girl in the door to the kitchenette. She wears a plain blue blouse with white stitching. A pack of cigarettes in the pocket over her huge left breast makes her look lopsided, unsteady. Soiled white short shorts, her

43

flabby thighs bulging unpleasantly from the legs of the shorts. Puffy face, mean green eyes. Her oak-colored hair is cut short, clotted in thick strands.

"There you are, Judy," says Preach.

"Mavis! Mavis, come here and look what the cat's drug in."

"Can't you turn that damn TV down?" asks Preach. Both of them have been shouting.

"Charles, I'm not going to tell you again," she hollers. The boy on the hassock leans and twists a knob.

"What you doin there, Mavis?" asks Preach.

She stands in the door, striking at her long brunette hair with a brush. Two hairpins in her mouth. She is wearing the same kind of blouse as Judy, but with matching slacks, and I see now that it is a uniform blouse. White sweat socks, black loafers. She is rather short, pretty except for a hardness in jaw line, and a sallow, washed eye. Lipstick printed over the edge of her upper lip to form a sickly Cupid's bow. She mumbles through the hairpins. "Preacher, you redheaded son of a bee-itch."

"Who's this feller?" asks Judy.

"This here's Jimmy Christopher," says Preach. "We come over in his car." No one has ever called me Jimmy.

"What'd you come for?"

"Well, goddamnit, I come to see you."

"I thought you'd know better after the way you carried on last time. And the cops out here and all. I thought you'd be smarter than to come back."

"Judy, you know they's nothin'll stop me from coming to see you."

"I know they's one something that will, and his name is Jack Davis."

"And where's he at, just tell me that."

44

"None of your beeswax," says Judy.

"He's still on the road," says Preacher. "He aint served his time out yet, that's where he is."

"That's all right," she says.

"I just thought we might go for a ride," he says.

"I wouldn't ride with you to a dog fight, the way you act."

The room is very hot. By now it is quite dark outside. Mavis has gone from the doorway, and now she is back, without the hairbrush and the pins. She leans in the door, watching Preacher and Judy.

"Well, I aint goin to beg you for nothing," says Preach. "If you-all gals are coming, you better come on. I don't intend to wait around here all night. I got better use for my time."

"We can't go nowhere till Mother comes home and puts these younguns to bed."

"Where's she at?"

"How should I know? She come off of her shift half an hour ago, but she aint here yet."

"Come on, Jimmy," says Preach. "We'll be back after a while."

"By God, you better be back," Judy says. "You stand me up and you'll *really* be in trouble, buddyro."

We go back out to the car. Preach opens the glove compartment and the toy firetruck falls out again. He throws it into the back seat. Both of us drink steadily for a few minutes. "Where to?" I ask him.

"We'll drag around a little and then we'll come on back," he says. "I just didn't want to have to put up with them damn kids today. They'll drive you crazy in a minute. That Charles, he's as mean as a snake with the toothache."

We go back to town and drive the main drag a couple of times. I see the same guy in the beer joint.

45

Then we drive out a couple of miles to a drive-in and eat sandwiches. The curb girl gives us an uninterested eye, although Preacher tries a couple of cracks on her. She's heard it all; she's heard everything, and she knows she has. But we sit for a while because Preach wants to hear "Mack the Knife" from the record box. The music comes out of the same speaker you tell your order into. The air is warm, without a breeze. There is a fuzzy haze about all the neon lights which pulls the dark sky down and wraps it tightly over the drive-in parking lot. When I put my head out the car window I can't see a single star.

When we get back to the house, some of the lights are out, and the television is turned off. The kids have been put to bed. We can hear an argument going among the girls in the living room.

"I don't care what you think about it," Judy is saying. "By God, I pay just as much on the rent and the groceries as anybody else around here. And I've got the right to do whatever I want. Me and Mavis owns just as much of this house as you do. If it wasn't for us helpin you out, you couldn't even live here." They don't stop because Preach comes in. "By God," she goes on, "I work as hard as you do. I ought to get to have a little fun. I put in my eight hours, and then I come home to mind them younguns. You aint got a thing you can say against me gettin out of this house just now and then."

She is talking to an older woman sitting across the room from her on a dingy wine-colored sofa. She looks as if she is in her mid-forties, with flaring dark hair, streaked with gray. She wears a mill uniform dress of gray cotton. She doesn't give Preacher or me a glance. "I just hope it don't get back to your husband," she says. "I just hope Jack Davis don't hear about it."

46

"He won't hear nothing," says Judy. "Just as long as you don't go buttin in to tell him."

"Come on if you're coming," says Preacher.

"Come on, Mavis," she says.

It's much cooler outside. I lurch a bit as the screen door slaps against me from Preacher's releasing it. This is the first time I notice that the liquor is affecting me. I'm rather surprised.

Mavis gets in silently without waiting for me to open the door for her. As Judy and Preacher get in the back seat, the toy firetruck falls out of the car. Preach kicks it skittering across the pavement. "Goddamnit, Jimmy," he says, "you're too old to be playing with toys." I get under the wheel and squirm around in the seat. "Where to?" I ask Preacher, keeping anger from my voice.

"Let's have us a drink first." He puts his hand on Judy's breast, and she slaps it away.

"Keep your goddamn hands to yourself," she says.

I hand the two bottles around. "There's not much left," I say.

"Places enough to get some though," says Preach. He peers through his bottle into the lights of an approaching car. "I know where's a pretty good place."

It is called Apex Longleaf Club, and I don't have the slightest notion where we are. Somewhere where the town lights of Apex are only a faint glow above a stand of pine trees. Long low building, oak siding stained red. Two long picture windows on either side of a white door. Both windows covered by drawn curtains: neon sign, BEER, in one. Gravel driveway, no neon advertising.

The place is fairly empty: three couples visible in the booths along the side. An acne-scarred waiter behind a

47

long, linoleum-covered bar. Garish jukebox against the right far wall.

The first thing Preach wants to do is to turn the jukebox louder. "I want to hear this 'Mashed Potatoes,' " he says.

The waiter says, "Preacher, what you doing up in this neck of the woods?"

"Just making the rounds." He pulls the box away from the wall and finds the volume switch.

"Damnit, Preach."

"Got to have some noise, Bill." He scratches his wiry red hair. "Hey, listen, man, did you ever sell that dog you had?"

"Nah," says Bill. "You know anybody interested in a good rabbit beagle?"

"Might," says Preacher. "Let me get another look at him." He goes around behind the counter, and he and the waiter go through a set of swinging doors.

I try to herd the girls to a booth as far as possible from the jukebox, but it's no go. "I want to sit where I can hear the music," says Judy. "And I bet Preacher does too." I slide in beside Mavis, Judy on the other side. "Are you one of Preacher's good buddies?" Judy asks me.

I shrug, and essay an answer of some sort: "No telling. You know how Preacher is."

"Lord, lord," she squeals. "That sure is the truth. He's the craziest thing, him. You can't tell one minute what he'll do the next. He's always up to something, aint he, Mavis?"

Mavis is twisting her dark hair around her finger. She doesn't open her mouth.

"How long have you-all known Preach?" I ask.

"Mm mnh. You know, I couldn't say," says Judy. "Except I believe it was right after my husband Jack

48

was sent on the roads the second time. Me and Mavis was at the drive-in movies by ourselves, and this car pulled up beside of us during the show. There was Preacher and this other real cute feller in it. What was his name? Wasn't his name Dick now, Mavis? But everybody called him Junior." She looked at me coyly —a disconcerting grimace. "He sure was real cute."

"What's your husband up for?"

"Oh, they said he broke into some store and stole a case of cigarettes. They always tell you some kind of lie like that. They don't like him because they know he don't like them and he don't care who knows it either. They're always pickin on him for something. I know he didn't steal them cigarettes, because he was workin then, and when they come out to the house and told him, he said, 'I never stole no cigarettes, but I'll pay for ever last one of em if it'll make you happy.' He said, 'Hell, them aint even my brand.'—That sure was funny that night," she says. I don't realize for a moment that she has changed the subject. "Preacher and that Junior pulled in beside of us, and Preacher leaned out of the window and said, 'Why don't you-all girls come and get in this car? Because it's got a better radio.' That just tickled me because here we was watchin a drive-in movie, and he wanted us to listen to the radio all the same time. I told him he sure was crazy, and he just said, 'Well, I'm sure you can do two things at once, can't you?' I was just tickled at that, you know what I mean?"

"Yes," I say, but I'm quite lost now. Her face indicates that I am to understand sexual innuendo in Preacher's remark, but I don't see it. I turn around to Mavis. "Was that the first time you met Preach, too?"

"I guess," she says vaguely, staring across the table at Judy.

49

Preacher returns, both pockets of the plaid sport jacket bulging. He hands me a paper bag with a bottle in it. "That dog's so fat he couldn't catch a rabbit in a tar pit," he says. "You owe me three dollars." Expensive, vile blended whiskey. Bill brings ice water and Seven-Up to our table. Preach is teasing and quarreling with and handling Judy. I ask Mavis if she would like to dance.

"I guess not."

In a short while, I'm fairly drunk, and they know it. Without looking, I can feel their eyes on my face. Now they're just waiting to see what I'll do. It seems to have become much warmer.

"How you doin there, Jimmy?" asks Preach.

"O.k." My voice sounds squeaky and gruff at once. My hands seem to have swelled; when I try to examine them, they come bobbing before my eyes like white balloons.

Judy moves out of the booth to go to the bathroom. Her receding buttocks flop in her tight shorts like basketballs in a flour sack. I watch myself flex my fingers and bend my hands at the wrist. The notion that it is not I who is doing it possesses me. I lean toward Preacher and whisper hoarsely. "For a long time now, someone else has been living my life. Or living in my life, inside. It's clear to me that I have been completely usurped."

"What's all that about?" he asks, grinning. It seems to me that his red hair really doesn't grow from his head, but floats and follows him about like a trained bird. Then I can't figure out who Preacher would be if his red hair didn't belong to him. I begin to look at my hands again, and it isn't a happy sensation. Something begins to rise in me. "Where's the john?" I ask.

Preacher points with his head. "You o.k.?"

Two curtains hung over an opening in the wall. I brush through them, and slam through a door on my right.

"Jesus Christ."

Here is Judy, squatting on the contraption like a huge bulbous frog. Her flabby skin like a frog's white belly. I fall backward through the swinging door. Another door on my left now, and I shove through it. It's still the wrong door. I feel that it's dark and cool, but I don't understand for a moment that I'm outside, staring at the back of the building. Whitewashed cement blocks. I lean forward, my hands against the blocks, and vomit three times. Four times.

Now I feel dizzier and lighter, but better. It's very cool. I look up to see stars, but there is a faint drizzle coming down, almost a spray. It feels good on my face. I kick about in the weedy lot here, swinging my arms. The lot borders a grove of tall pine trees, as dark and silent as a great cave. A path runs through the weeds and into the woods, and I strike along it, hoping that the damp walk will jar logic awake in my head. It's very dark, but I try to examine the contents of my pockets as I walk along: wrinkled soiled handkerchief and a folded clean one, pocketknife, rather hefty handful of change, car keys, cigarettes, matches, ball-point pen. I throw away the soiled handkerchief, wipe my face and neck with the clean one.

A vague grayish light behind the trees ahead. The woods odors much more intense now. The trees fall away and a rather large pond appears. I see a boat on the low bank about twenty feet to my right, and I go to sit in it. It is brighter here, with the pond reflecting the little light that there is in the sky. The pond laps against the bank with a sound like a barber stropping a straight razor.

It's all terribly muddled now. I take out my wallet and strike a match and count my money. Twelve dollars. Change amounting to one dollar seventy-three cents. I light a cigarette before I toss the match away. I feel much better now, but not entirely safe. The urgent need to form a plan presses me, but it's difficult to gather myself. At last I strike another match and search through the cards in my wallet until I find the Code of Conduct. ONE: *I am an American fighting man. . . .* No. Two: *I will never surrender of my own free will. If in command I will never surrender my men while they still have the means to resist.* Still no go; I have never understood number two, but it has always seemed important. THREE: *If I am captured I will continue to resist by all means available. I will make every effort to escape and aid others to escape. I will accept neither parole nor special favors from the enemy.* This is better; I feel some response stirring in me. I think that I ought to be able to set something up here. FOUR: *If I become a prisoner of war, I will keep faith with my fellow prisoners. I will give no information or take part in any action which might be harmful to my comrades. If I am senior, I will take command. If not, I will obey the lawful orders of those appointed over me and will back them up in every way.* Now it is clear enough. I read on to the end of the code, but it is apparent that rules three and four are the ones which are applicable. I let my last view of Judy rise in my mind. Think of hot flesh as fat as jelly, sweating and farting. It is obvious; I must accept no favors, I must keep faith.

Out in the pond I hear a couple of splashes. Bass jumping in the night. A man-shaped form comes out of the woods, following the path. It comes toward me, attracted by my glowing cigarette.

"That you, man?" Preacher.

"Here I am." I jump out of the boat.

It's hard to make out his features in the gloomy light. "Look, man, you had us all shook up." He comes and puts his hand on my arm. "You all right?"

"Yes."

"What you doin out here by your damn self?"

I think. "Just resting," I say.

"Well," he says, "we better get back. Them gals'll be missing us. You got them all worried about you, man."

Except for our party and Bill the barkeeper, the place is empty now. As soon as she sees me, Judy begins to snort and giggle. "You sort of got in the wrong pew, didn't you?" she asks.

I just shake my head as if I were embarrassed and not frightened.

"You son of a bee-itch," says Mavis. I sit beside her, not understanding what she intends by the epithet. She doesn't sound angry.

"Here, man," says Preach, "have you a drink. Mavis aint drunk it all yet."

"Not right now," I say. "I think I'll just have a beer."

"I don't like beer when I'm dating," says Preacher. "It puts me out of the mood."

Judy coughs and giggles. "I swear you're a crazy damn thing," she says to Preach.

It goes on like that for another hour.

Two-thirty in the morning. Judy says, "I don't know what Mavis thinks, but I'm going home. I've got to get up tomorrow for a seven-o'clock shift, and I'm goin to get me some sleep before I go in that hosery mill."

53

"Oh hell," says Preach. "It's still early. It's just a little after one."

"Don't give me that," she says. "It's three o'clock if it's a minute. I can't gallivant around the whole night like you. I've got a eight-hour shift to make. I've got two mouths to feed, besides myself."

"You don't have to go in tomorrow," he says.

"I've done told you I've got two kids," she says.

"Well," he says, "that's what you get for sleeping on your back."

No response. She has turned off the machine for the night; she's tired, needs sleep, determined to be cross until she gets to bed.

I am driving, but I don't know where we are: one of those interminable asphalt-and-gravel roads that run through pine forests and over occasional bridges. Yellow road signs flutter in the headlights and fly away like huge moths. Grassy road shoulder melting by like a green river . . . Mavis leans against the door, peering ahead. She wishes for a radio in the car.

"Is there any place you can get to from here?" I ask.

"You goddamn well better be able to get me home from here," says Judy. Her voice is dead, a sound like two sticks struck together. "Aint that so, Mavis?"

"I guess," says Mavis.

"All right, then," says Preach, "if that's the way you feel about it." He leans forward so that I can hear him. "Turn around the next chance you get," he says. "I'll show you from there."

5

IT IS ALMOST four o'clock in the morning when I park the car before my house. The cool drizzle has stopped. Everything is damp and steamy. The clouds are rifting apart now, like skim ice breaking up in a puddle, and acidulous moonlight seeps into the grain of things. My body is rancid with dried sweat and fear. Quiet as sleep, the suburban street is patched with the dim light. The hood of the car ticks with dissipated heat after I cut the motor.

I sneak into the house, the floor squeaking under me, my skin tickling in anticipation of smashing into unseen furniture. In the living room, I settle wearily, but not sleepily, into the flowered easy chair nearest the door. The window in the south wall pours the stained moonlight on the drab rug. From the children's bedroom, I hear breathing march and halt as they stir crossly under the prodding of their dreams. I light a cigarette. My wife rises from the sofa across the room and comes to me. She is barefoot; her hair is down, and she wears a thick cotton bathrobe. She stands before me where I sit, seeming tall and heavy in the darkness.

"James?"

"Yes."

She places her hand, cool with waiting, on my head and rumples my hair. "Are you all right?"

"How long have you been waiting?"

"Not long," she says, lying. "Is it very bad? It really is, isn't it?"

"I'm all right."

"Coffee or anything?"

"No."

"Come on to bed."

I lift a corner of her bathrobe and press it to my face. The soft cotton is warm, slightly musky, the odor of woman and boudoir. Her white legs shine in the dark. I place my desireless hand behind her left knee. Her flesh is very warm, almost hot, and I realize that to her my hand must be as cold as frozen metal. I retrieve my dropped cigarette from the rug. "Not yet," I say.

"It's very late," she whispers.

"You go on," I say. "I'll be there in a little while. You go on."

"Well, then." She moves away, clasping the robe about her with both long hands. In a few minutes I hear the springs as she climbs into bed. *Tuck*, she sets the clock alarm; *pump, pump*, she shapes the pillow.

It is almost completely silent. Then a mockingbird begins in the sycamore in the back yard. In the silence, the song sounds loud enough to break windows and to smash locks. Far off, the faint bark of a tied dog. I can even hear my body rubbing the insides of my clothes as I breathe.

I go into my study and turn on the light. The dusty messiness comforts me: here are the pulp magazines, the cheap books, the manuscript out of order where my sister displaced the pages. I am grateful to Sylvia for not having cleaned the room. I decide to make coffee, and go into the kitchen. When I try to open a new can of coffee, the key slips and the opening ring of metal gets twisted. I begin to sweat again, and I can't get the thing started right. Finally, I wrap the loose tin around

56

my palm and pull the top open. My hand is ripped, sticky with blood. No pain; only a dry numbness. I feel the surges of sickness, my stomach a cramped fist, but I have nothing left to throw up. I hold my bleeding right hand over the sink and try to fix the coffee with my left. I get the percolator plugged in at last, although I have dumped about a quarter of the can into the coffeemaker. Patches of sweat on my shirt, my hands trembling like shaken wires. The percolator gurgles like someone strangling.

I wait until the coffee is made. Reaching into the cupboard, I drop a saucer on the drainboard of the sink. Finally I get a cup poured, and bend to pick up as much china as I can so that the children won't get cut. I throw the splinters into the sink, and carry the cup carefully in both hands back to the study and set it on the table. Part of the cup I spill, hitting it with my elbow as I sit down. I decide that next time will be better; I will get a whole cup of coffee.

I pile through the stuff on my desk, looking for what I need to read. I come across *I, Robot*. I can't remember the four laws of robotics. *A robot cannot kill a human being* . . . and what else? I begin to read the book, then with a pencil I note on the back of a page of the manuscript another book I must reread. I turn back to the story at hand.

Sylvia's white face above, nearing and receding like an animal bounding against a wall of rubber. Demon hid in a cloud.

"James. James. Are you all right? Let me see."

"See. What?"

"Are you all right? Let me see."

I raise my head from the desk. When I try to scratch

my neck, a sheet of paper rasps my cheek. I'm stuck to the paper. It shows a ghost-shaped red stain where I have bled. I pull it away and read the penciled title of a book: *The Human Use of Human Beings.*

"Hello," I say. Something mean and stupid squats in my brain.

"I was afraid," says Sylvia. "I saw the blood and glass in the kitchen. It's all over everything. Are you hurt?"

"I'm all right."

"Is it your hand? Let me see." She opens my hand gently, pulling back a finger at a time, like peeling a banana. A broad red lash across the palm.

"Come on in the bathroom." She tugs me by my left arm.

"Where are the kids?"

"They've already started to play, even before breakfast." She turns to me, smiling, a lump of cotton in her hand. "Here," she says. She holds my hand over the lavatory, dabbing at the dried blood.

"I dropped a saucer," I said. "I'm sorry."

She is very cheerful. "That's all right," she says. "It was chipped anyway, and I had already broken one of the cups. So really we just have a full set now." She holds my hand higher, to get the light on the cut. "Look," she says, "it's not too deep. But that's really annoying, to have it across your right hand like that."

"It's o.k.," I say.

She flicks me a quick glance. "I've already got some new coffee making. The stuff in the pot was black as pitch."

I go to the open back door of the kitchen and look through the screen at the kids playing in the yard. The plastic wading pond is dry and they have filled it with toys. John is four. He takes a toy train from the wading pond and sets it on the ground. "Here is the choochoo train," he says. "Here is the train, coming along. Choo, choo, choo."

Missy is two. "Choo choo," she says feverishly. "Choo! CHOO!"

"How do you want your eggs?" asks Sylvia.

"Any way you have yours," I say.

After breakfast I feel better, but wobbly and empty, like a capsized boat. I'm out of cigarettes.

"The people at the press called yesterday afternoon," Sylvia says. "They wanted to know if you could help with an estimate on a new book."

"I'm going to take a nap," I say.

I wake up about three o'clock, and decide that for lunch I want corned beef and beer. At the delicatessen I run into Ike Amos, whom I roomed with my second year in college. I haven't seen him since. It turns out that he is married now, no kids, working as a trainee in paper inspection for the Government Printing Office. Long, serious face, hidden eyes.

"I never figured you as a production manager," he says. "You were always talking politics. I thought you'd be a lawyer or something."

"No. I don't even read the newspaper now," I say.

6

A LITTLE BEFORE eight o'clock I'm helping Sylvia wash the dishes from the evening meal. The wall telephone in the kitchen rings and she answers. "Hello. Hello. Anybody there?" She hangs it up, puzzled but not angry. "Whoever it was wouldn't talk," she says.

"That's always scary," I say, banging pans into the drawer in the electric stove.

"I could hear them breathing over the phone."

"Just a wrong number."

"They ought to apologize, then." She pulls the sink drain and the plane of suds recedes slowly, like Atlantis sinking. "James, could you do me a favor and fix the knob on the back door here?"

"Sure." I look at the lock. Nothing to fix except to tighten the set screws in the knob to stop its slipping around on the shaft. I feel disappointed that the problem is not greater. I remember that one of the last questions on a psychological test I once took—it was the Minnesota Multiphase Personality Inventory, a standard test—was: *Would you be happy to spend your life repairing door locks?* I answered in the affirmative, and now it occurs to me that I cannot understand a person who would not answer *yes*. But, when I think, I cannot find among my friends a single person who would answer *yes*. I recognize this problem as the kind which gives me a headache, and I resolve to put it out of my mind. "That'll hold the knob," I say, and toss the screwdriver into my cloth tool bag. "Anything on TV tonight?"

Sylvia peels off her yellow rubber gloves and drapes them over the spigot. "Oh, James. What is it you want? What do you care about it? What is it you want me to do?"

"I'm all right," I say. "I'm just resting."

She stares at me, her cheeks white and quivering. Her eyes boil up with tears, which break and run on her face.

"Honey," I say.

"I don't know," she cries, holding her left wrist in her right hand and twisting it first one way, then back. "I don't know what you want. We never used to get phone calls like that. They've called four or five times today like that, and wouldn't talk."

"It's kids, then, playing with the telephone."

"It's somebody I don't know. They're waiting for you to answer. They won't talk to me."

I keep on shaking my head *no*. "I don't believe that's right."

She gives two deep sighs to recover from her crying. Turning away from me, she rubs her face with her hands. I look at her slender back, clenching with gulped sobs under the paisley print blouse. She is in shorts, and her long slender legs are very white under the fluorescent kitchen light. "I'm sorry," she murmurs.

"It's nothing to be frightened of," I say. "Next time, just let me answer the phone. I'll put a stop to it."

She turns about with a timorous smile. "I'm sorry. It's nothing to get upset about; I know it."

"Here, I'll fix you a Coke." I squeeze a lemon quarter into it as she likes. "Let's go into the living room," I say.

She nestles into a chair, knees against her breasts,

61

bare heels caught on the edge of the chair cushion. She rubs the back of the chair with her head; lamplight spills in her dark-blond hair. "All right," she says, "but don't let's watch television. Let's just talk."

After this it's no good, of course. I can't think of anything to ask about the kids. I can't stop my eyes resting on the blank TV screen or on the tight door to my study. She sips at her Coke in anticipatory silence. Here are both of us in a rather small living room which needs repainting. The white door is stained, at thigh level, with dirt from the kids' hands. Four pieces of furniture to sit upon, a plastic hassock, a two-piece hi-fi set with a crammed record case, a well-beaten coffee table, two stuffed bookcases, two precisely aligned rows of pictures on opposite walls, the floor and drab rug spangled with red toys: but it's as desolate and frightening and immense as the desert at noon. She waits. I wait.

"Did I tell you they called from the press about an estimate on a new book?" she asks.

"Let's go for a ride," I say.

"The children."

"They'll be o.k. They never wake up. Anyway, we won't be gone that long. Just to get some cool air."

"Let me make up."

While she sits at the mirror in the bedroom, I switch the television on. Family situation comedy. Smart Little Bastard: "Aw gee, Dad, just this once. Can't I, please, Dad, huh?" Dad, with his wise pipe fuming philosophically: "Son, there's one thing you have to learn sooner or later. A fellow can't always have things just the way he wants them. When you learn this you've taken a big step toward becoming a real man." Pause, with kindly glance. "But maybe just this once wouldn't hurt. You and your mother get together, and if she says you may, then you have my permission too." Smart L.B., with cheesecake grin and bug eyes: "Gee thanks, Dad! She already said it was o.k. with her if it was o.k. with you." Darts out of the room. For no apparent reason, a volley of canned laughter.

"Ready, hon?" I follow her out to the car and open the door for her.

We pull out of our suburban street to the intersection of Alpine Avenue, a main thoroughfare full of light and noise. It's strange to think of our own house, only two blocks behind us, white and still under the somnolent elms which line the street. And in the still house, my silent study with its queer documents strewn about like living things suspended in a sudden trance. I nose the car into the roaring street.

I follow the stream of traffic a few blocks, and then turn, on a sudden impulse, onto College Drive. Winton College looms on our right: gray stone buildings with few lights showing. I look toward the third floor of one of the largest buildings. The windows of the office where I worked are black. A solitary campus cop stands in the lighted doorway of the building. Slowly he looks about him, tests the door, finds it satisfactorily locked, hitches at his scrotum. School is out for the spring; summer session hasn't yet begun. I remember that I still have keys to the building and to the office. I make two left turns, circling the campus; stare fascinated, as at a dead body.

Then back into Alpine: lights, horns, brakes; the restless Brownian movement of aimless traffic. I have the quick feeling that this night and every night all America is scurrying the black roads, I with the rest. In an hour, if we could find the great right road, we could leave all the houses empty, the land deserted. A white '59 Chevrolet, hood ornament missing, slung low in the hindquarters, dashes past me and then slows to thirty. Trying to pick a race. The lights of approaching cars show me the shape of a boy's head, the big fuzzy dice dangling from the rear-view mirror. I follow quietly until he zips off in search of an answer to his challenge.

"How do you think I'd go in a ducktail haircut?" I ask Sylvia.

"Pretty silly."

"How about a bushy beard and a top hat?"

She laughs, almost easily, and puts her hand on my knee. "Very masculine," she says. "Very nice."

I pull into a drive-in, and we have fried onion rings and milkshakes. Couples quarreling and snuggling in the glary cars. Loud bad music. The bandage on my hand looks blond-tinged under the pink neon. As I pull out of the lot, my right front fender smashes against the right rear fender of a black Dodge which is pulling into the drive-in. I can tell it's not serious, and I pull away as fast as I can turn the wheel, and race down the street. Glimpse of a girl's startled face over her steering wheel.

"Stop, James," Syliva cries. "Stop. It was her fault."

The short hair on the back of my neck is prickly with sweat. "We've got to get home," I say. "The children are all alone."

"It was her fault," she says. "I'm sure it was. There'll be trouble if you don't go back."

A dull roaring in my ears; inside the roar, as in a box, a sound like a handsaw cutting into a pine knot. My wrists are weak; I feel that I can't control the car. "We've got to get home where it's quiet," I say. Someone blows an angry horn as I run a red light. "I don't have a license."

Sylvia stares out the side window. I'm driving too

close to the curb. "What happened? Where is your license?"

"Expired . . . I couldn't take the test." I stop the car before the house. A violent tic in my left eyelid; still the dull roar. "I couldn't take the test to have it renewed. I don't know anything about it."

She puts her hand on my forearm and finds the cold sweat. "Honey, honey." The bad weight of my loud breathing. "Let's go in. I'll fix something."

We go in on tiptoe. It's very quiet. Sylvia brings me water and two aspirins. I take the aspirins and drink all the water and follow her into the kitchen, where she begins to make hot chocolate. It's better now. I watch her abstractedly. When the telephone rings, I jerk as if I had been touched with hot iron.

"Hello. Hello. Hello," I say.

"Jimmy? . . . Is that you, Jimmy?" Judy's voice.

"Don't call back here again." My voice is hoarse and wobbly. I hang up the receiver. Sylvia avoids looking at me as she hands me the chocolate.

"There's a western on the late show," she says. "Robert Mitchum, I think."

I feel much better when the screen blooms with movement. I lean forward and stare unblinking. During one of the commercial breaks, she says, "Don't worry. I'll go down to the police station tomorrow. I'll tell them I was driving." I nod mutely.

The movie still has about ten minutes to run when she says, yawning, "I just can't stay up. I'm sorry, really I am, but I'll have to get up early with the kids."

"You shouldn't apologize. I should, not you."

"No," she says. "I have to."

I even watch "The Star-Spangled Banner," the picture of the flag waving and the chorus singing, before cutting off the set and going into my study.

65

In here it's like being swathed in cotton. I pull at random a sheet from the typed manuscript. *Take yourself up,* it says. *My sermon* . . . "Shit." I jerk a novel out of the jumble. Here is *The Island of Dr. Moreau.*

7

ONE WHOLE SUMMER I fought with Hurl, Uncle's boy. Hurl had the comically sad face of one of Uncle's hungriest hounds, and a body rather like a daddy-longlegs: a short concave trunk, with long, thin arms and legs. His head dipped forward, so that he always had to look up at the people he encountered from beneath a troubled, dirty brow. It was like a hermit peering out of a cave. I was older than he, but it didn't make any difference. The first time he caught me alone—we had been sent to the farthest corner of the pasture to find out if a cow had calved—he turned to me and muttered sadly, "I can whip your ass."

"You've got it to prove," I said.

He gave me a gentle push to discover whether I was made of flesh or wood, and I struck him with my doubled fist, my whole strength behind the blow. He merely looked still more sad and pelted me with punches until my nose bled and my eyes watered and my ears hummed. I sobbed in frustration because I couldn't get to his squat body: it was like trying to hit a pygmy hidden behind a windmill. Finally I begged him to stop.

"Say calf rope."

"Damn you anyhow," I said. "You don't fight fair." I rushed at him, and it began again. "Calf rope. Calf rope," I said. Then I said "you son of a bitch" under my breath, and he kicked me down the hill.

67

"Don't you never forget I can whip your ass," he said.

The next time, we were in the cornfield, hoeing the way my grandmother prescribed. This way to hoe was a pretty complex operation: first we had to chop away the weeds from both sides of the corn plant, then we had to cut the weeds from between this row and the next one over, then we had to dig around, loosening a great handful of dirt to heap about the root of the plant. This latter habit she called "making hills." Now it was mid-June and the corn was a bit taller than our ankles. We were supposed to be hoeing with my grandmother, who was already three or four rows ahead of us.

"You didn't make that hill right," I told Hurl. "You just pulled big clods on top of that corn, without breaking them up."

"Let me alone," he said. "This aint no way to hoe corn nohow."

"It's the way we've got to do," I said, "and you aren't doing it right."

"I'll do the way I want," he said. "Because I can still whip your ass."

This time we wrestled. Somehow I threw him and crawled on top, trying to get my knees on his shoulders. But he rolled me over in a flash and wallowed me a good long time, beating my face with his fist each time he got a chance. At last I managed to stand up and locked his head against my right side with both arms.

Whack. My grandmother struck me squarely across my back with the handle of her hoe. "What are you doing? You stand back."

It burned painfully where she hit me, and I thought that I could feel the welt rising already. "That hurt," I complained.

"Well, sir," she said. "It isn't more than the least you deserve. Just look what you trifling boys have done. And you, sir"—myself—"aren't you ashamed to be fighting somebody younger and smaller than you are?"

Hurl said, "Aw, I can whip his ass."

"And just look around you at the corn you've wallowed down. It may be that you young men have become too good to eat cornbread, but the rest of us haven't." A sudden softening melted her voice. "Son, now, you must watch, and not fight any more."

It was true. The tender stalks were trampled and ichorous, and the day's hoeing had just begun.

Another time we were in the hayfield. The open field roared with heat and work and the singing of insects. Tall, cool trees bordered the field on all sides, and locusts sang in them. Hurl and I were snaking in the hay. I was riding the horse, while Hurl went from hayshock to hayshock, waiting for me. When I brought the horse slowly back, the cotton line trailing and bobbling in the sharp stubble, he looped the line closely about the bottom of the shock and tied it to a short chain. Then I dragged the shock to the place where the fierce men were building the haystack. When I brought in the last shock before lunch, Hurl rode it, draping his arms over one side, his legs over the other, like a dead man.

Uncle stood by the half-built stack, drinking warm, dusty water from a quart canning jar. Water dripped from his mouth, blackening his overalls, trickling down his shirt. He held the jar toward Hurl and me. "Want some?" We didn't. "Well, that's fine." He took off his stained baseball cap and dumped the rest of the water over his head. He slapped the wet hair out of his face. "That'll just make me itch good," he said. To Hurl: "Unhitch Monroe from that shock. I ain't goin to throw another bite of hay till I've eat my dinner." I jumped gladly off the horse and pulled at my dungarees. I ached badly from having ridden for a day and a half the horse's steely backbone.

To eat our lunch we went to a clump of sassafras that had sprung up about a stump in the center of the field. My mother had packed biscuits and salty ham, cold boiled corn, a whole tomato. We all finished with buttermilk and spring onions that Uncle had brought. "You get out here and work a while and even a poke dinner tastes good," he told me. He looked at me blankly for a space; his eyes were always opaque. "Hurl tells me he can whip you," he said. "I don't reckon it's the truth, though, because Hurl will lie you like a rug on the floor."

"I don't believe he can," I said.

"I can whip your ass any time," Hurl said.

This time it didn't take so long because by now I knew he could. I didn't put up much fight.

"I guess it's the truth then," said Uncle, rolling a Prince Albert cigarette, "but I wouldn't never of believed it."

By late August the barn was always filled with hay. The rains came, the hard glare of lightning stretching the heavy air and snapping it back. Sometimes, but not too often, there would be hail which would strip the tobacco stalks, leaving the broad leaves but tarry rags. The creek would swell and redden, flooding the fields at times, leaving streaks of white gravel on the dark loam. The ditches altered their shapes, became deeper and harder. Goldenrod burst out, and the fences and roadsides were splotched with long rows of it, nodding heavily in the full breeze. Hard, sweet apples knotted the limbs. The last calves were born. We could tell that fall was coming. The nights were still hot, but the early mornings began to pinch.

My room in the big brick house was an upstairs bedroom which faced west, two gable windows giving on the sunset. Directly across, a hill slumped steeply toward the farm, and then a stretch of pasture and marshy bottom verged on our fences. Through the center, Trivet's Creek ran placidly. The room was walled with pine slatting, streaked like bacon. A number of shelves filled with pulp magazines and cheap paperbound books were on the wall by the door. Two huge beds, with mattresses hard as oak, sat at right angles. Between them a black table stood, holding my rusty typewriter, piles of correspondence, sheaves of poems, and a kerosene lamp by which I wrote.

Among the poems on my desk was the never-to-be-finished epic of the Ironbird, a long, unrhymed, non-metrical poem about a bird whose wings were door hinges, whose brain was an abacus, whose tail was a poker hand of cards. This bird flew round the world twice daily. It could see into the far past and the far future, prophesying in unintelligible language. It preached against the horrible sin of cannibalism.

Also on the black desk were messages from my grandmother, which took multitudinous and protean forms. A great many of these communications were simply newspaper clippings which she left for me on my pillow, where she left all her notes. No common theme characterized these clippings: they ranged from the daily "two-minute sermons" to archaeological discoveries to baseball and football scores. There were also reminders about my grooming: "Son you must slick your hair down with this oil and not go bush headed," one read; another might be about a mouthwash. Moral instruction: "Son I think maybe you are reading too low and sinful writing. Please remember the Bible is best of all."

Other notes were simply lists of tasks she wanted me to do without delay. All her messages dangled from a finishing nail I had driven into the corner of the desk, a painful record of all the time she spent thinking about me.

The work lists were more numerous than the other messages. She never stopped working and expected no one else to stop. Sometimes at midnight, or even two in the morning, I heard her banging the heavy steel milk cans from the dairy as she washed them. And it was she who called me early in the morning, sometimes at four o'clock, to work. "Whooee, son. Time, now. Time to get up and get started. Whooee." Many times she must have worked the day, the night, and the day.

"The trouble is, she won't quit herself and she don't want you to quit," Uncle said. We were sitting on the back porch of his house, the weathered tenant house, late in the long August afternoon. The sky bulged with dark clouds, the air was leaden with the coming rain. "She can work any man down I ever heard tell of. And not by tellin him nothin, either. Just by waitin and waitin until he's workin at three or four things at one time. About half the time she's waitin for you to tell what's in her mind so you can jump to work on that, too."

"I know she can work me down without half trying," I said. "It doesn't trouble her."

"Main thing, is chinchiness," said Uncle. "Now, you take when she's on a haystack and it's just about built. It's about twenty foot high by then, and it's all I can do to punch that hay up to her. But she stands up there on top, havin a hold on that stack pole, and she'll point you out a place. 'Whooee,'" he was mimicking, "'put a little dab there, mister. Now a little dab over here.' That's what'll wear a man down, in a minute."

72

"It's goin to storm," said Hurl, looking apprehensively at the white undersides of the leaves furling in the breeze. He was sitting on the floor of the porch, hunched over the repairing of an irremediably crippled .22 rifle.

"I aint never seen anything like it," Uncle said. "Here is this big overgrowed toad frog of a boy scared of a little thunder."

"It's a danger," Hurl said. "I don't see why you aint been struck fifty times the way you stay out in it."

"I never seen the beat," Uncle said. He turned back to me. "Now you wait, when that corn's ready to pull, they'll be some certain way she wants it piled in the crib. Not just throw it in and shut it up, but put it in some certain way. That's what it is that eats a man up, that chinchy stuff."

"Like the way she wants it hoed," I said. "It takes forever. And I can't see the good of it."

"Well, it's the way she is." He crossed his legs, the cane-bottomed chair creaking. "But I'll tell you what: if she told me to get on the barn roof and jump off and fly like a flibbertijibbet"—he meant a helicopter—"I'd do it. I wouldn't say *Yes mam* or *No mam*, I'd just start climbin."

A blue gash in the clouds, and the thunder started, like an empty barrel rolled down a flight of stairs. Hurl darted into the house; the screen door banged after him. Uncle and I sat silent; flies gathered on the porch about us. His eyes were opaque, his face impassive. "I never seen the beat," he said finally. "A long overgrowed boy. He's in there hidin under the bed."

I kept quiet.

"Reach me that broom handle," said Uncle. "I never seen such a baby."

We went into the earthy-smelling bedroom and Uncle poked the broom under the bed and rattled it around until he found resistance. Then he punched vigorously with it. Hurl emitted squeals and curses. "Goddamn you," he cried. "Quit jobbin me. Leave me alone."

"I never seen such a baby," Uncle said. "Come on out from under that bed."

The house rattled with a blast of thunder, and the first gust of rain boomed on the tin roof. The thin glass shook in the window frames. Suddenly the broom was jerked from Uncle's hand and it disappeared under the bed. "Goddamn your eyes," Hurl squeaked. "I wouldn't come out from under this bed for a hunderd dollars."

Uncle regarded the worn crazyquilt which covered the bed, his hands locked behind the bib of his overalls. "Well," he said to me, "let's go out on the porch where it's cool."

8

"CHECK," said my grandfather.

It was bishop's gambit. I had already castled, and there was nothing I could move. I stared at the board for a long time. "Look," I said, suddenly excited. With my finger hovering, moving in the air above the pieces, I traced a pointed form, the shape of a beech leaf.

He leaned back, his green eyes sharp on my finger, then on my face. "I can't understand you," he said. "A feller can't never tell where your mind's at."

The loud clock scratched and set to strike.

Outside, a powdery snow spat in the black night, and the December wind scrabbled over the wood shingles of my father's house. A thin red cotton blanket draped around me, I sat shivering and sniveling on the sagging bed upstairs. The tiny room was bare, except for the bed and the single straight chair in the corner, where my father sat, his gray eyes lancing me. The wallpaper was yellow, with a lace design. A single bulb screwed in the low ceiling shed a hard, cold light.

In the small room, my father seemed as huge as a bear. He sat leaning forward, his elbows on his knees. His square, fleshy face was hard as granite, his features set in a determined, sadly grave expression. He never took his full eyes off me. "How old are you?" he asked.

"Nine," I said. "Nine and a half." I felt cold and hot

at once, fevered, frightened, and angry.

"Fine," he said. "That means you know how old nine years old is, and it means you can tell good from bad in a minute, because it's bound to be clear black and white to you. You couldn't have done enough thinking yet to get you mixed up." His voice was large and hot, and rubbed my mind like a file. "Nine. And if you'd set out, as I think you must have done, to break your grandfolks' hearts from the minute you were born, you couldn't have done a better job than you already have in the past few months. I'm taking it for granted —and don't you say a word, because I don't want to know whether I'm right or wrong—that you didn't set fire to their house on purpose."

"I didn't mean—"

He flicked his right hand. "You hush; hush up. It's still a fact, whatever you had in mind, and nobody I know can help me with that either, that the house is almost completely ruined. More than that, I'm going to take it for granted that you don't know what it meant to your mother's daddy and mother to have been living in the house as a third generation. Your grandfather's grandfather built that house, and he was an old man then. Your grandfather has remodeled it twice, keeping the place up, keeping it sound for the next generation —which is your mother and me—and the generation after us, which is you or your sister. It was your grandfather's father who made a brick house out of it at a time when there weren't two brick houses in this county, having to have them sent from Atlanta, Georgia, in a boxcar, and then having to haul them out here in a horse-drawn wagon on roads not as good as a bog path. I'm going to take it for granted that you didn't know or didn't understand what that meant to them, even though you've heard them talk about the house

76

and their folks all your life."

"Yes sir," I said. I remembered the long descant about the house, about relatives, about the old times, which my grandmother and grandfather divided between them by the cheering stove, eternally talking, as if unwinding a never-ending ball of yarn.

"Hush," he said, lifting his hand. "I don't want to hear any admission from you. I want to hope you're not any worse than the worst I can imagine about you right now. I'm going to believe that you don't understand the feeling of having a real past that you can remember and remember hearing about. I'm going to make myself believe that you're feeble-minded, an idiot, and not ready for or capable of the company of anyone else. In fact, I'm going to believe that you don't know that anything in the world is important except having your belly full and your hide warm and Santa Claus. The only other choice I've got besides that is that you're an evil person. I'd rather believe the other because you're too young for me to stand to watch you grow up if it is true and you are purposely evil." He fell into silence, staring before him unblinkingly, as if he had just discovered an unknown species of animal. I opened my mouth to say something, and he jerked abruptly into talk. "And about the lie: you said you saw a redheaded man sneaking around the corner of the house and then you went to sleep and when you woke up the house was already on fire. All of that's a lie. In the first place, when your grandmother sent you into the back bedroom, she said she would be in in a little while. She was going to sleep in there with you so she could know if you got too cold in the night. But when you went to bed, you kept on all your clothes and even your shoes. Now, you had matches and a cigarette and you were going to try to learn to smoke . . ."

77

"No sir," I said, "I wasn't . . ."

"Shut up. I'm not going to think that you were lying there in bed with all your clothes on, playing with matches. So: you found out you didn't like smoking and didn't think to put out a live cigarette and it got away from you and burned its way into the mattress where no power in the world could stop it from burning. But you tried to put it out, and ran back and forth from the bathroom with glasses of water. So, you were scared then, but not scared enough to tell your granddaddy and grandmother until the flames started up and the fire had a good head start. You were still so scared of your punishment—let me say that you were so scared because you thought the proper punishment for you for starting the fire was to be hung or to be put in jail— that when you went to tell your grandfolks you told them the lie about seeing the redheaded man first, *then* you told them that the house was on fire."

He was silent a long while. I sat shivering under the blanket, hugging my chest with my cold arms.

Then he went on. "And, since I've got this far, I can believe the rest without any trouble. That it took you so long to tell your story that by the time you were finished lying you were scared of the fire itself then more than anything else. And that's why you ran out of the house by yourself, without helping the old folks out at all.—Well"—he stopped to light a cigarette, and leaned back in the straight chair—"that's the fairy tale I've made up for myself. Your mother and your grandparents will make up one to suit themselves. I'm probably the only one of us who knows that it is a fairy tale. I can't tell if I'm lucky or unlucky. . . .

"I'm sure you don't care about any of this, what I think or what they think. All you want to know is what's going to happen to you, what kind of punishment you've got to look forward to. But you don't need to worry, there's not going to be any punishment. There's only going to be a new schedule. The only thing that's going to hurt is your backbone." He paused, pondering. "If you've got one."

I was ill for two days, shuddering in the bare room alone. Then the new regimen began. My father's gruff hand shook me awake every morning at four-thirty, and we went together through the bitter cold to the barn to milk. At first I didn't know enough to warm my hands before touching the teats, so that I was kicked viciously two or three times. Then, while my father carried the milk to the house, leaving me a pailful to bring, I turned the cows out of the barn into the white pasture and threw hay over the fence to them. They crowded and butted to get at the first forkfuls. Then, if it had been very cold during the night, I went with a hatchet over the snowy hills to the watering pond for the cattle and chopped up the ice so that drink might be accessible. Then I carried the milk home, washed, and ate breakfast, went upstairs and made my bed and set my room in order. If there was still time before the hour to walk to school, I was to shine every shoe in sight, or to do whatever my mother might ask me to. After school, I dressed in overalls and smelly milking coat again and went out to count the steers in the fields where the summer corn had grown, and I walked the road and creek bank, inspecting the fences. "If one of these calves gets out, you're the one to answer for it," my father had said. "They're all your responsibility now, and I wish there were a thousand of them." Then until the evening milking time I was to shuck corn for the two horses, Monroe and Jackson, and to shell corn for

79

the chickens, and to throw hay for the evening down into the mangers from the loft. There was usually some time left over before milking time—there just wasn't that much to do in the winter—but my father had ordered my grandparents not to allow me into the house until after the evening milking. I lay in the hay and thought and dreamed; soon I began to smuggle books out to the loft, hiding them in my underwear. After milking I helped pour the milk up and strain it, and I set the heavy cans out for the truck driver from the dairy to pick up. After supper I was to study my schoolwork for two hours. "Study is what you'll be doing, too," my father had said, "because I'm going to be right in the room with you. I don't imagine you study two hours a week now, and I don't suppose you can think how you're going to study for two hours a day. But if you're so fast that you finish the books beforehand, you can start on them again at the beginning." He sat across from me in the steamy kitchen, reading the news or grading his students' papers. After study I had half an hour to do with as I liked: to read books he approved, or to listen to the radio if he didn't mind my having it on.

He found me reading *Ungava Bob*. "Did you finish your arithmetic?"

"Yes sir."

He flipped the book over and looked at the green spine. "What's this about?" he asked, his voice lazy and absent.

"It's about a trapper in Alaska," I said, "and he gets chased by wolves in one part. That's a good part."

Holding the book spread in his left hand, he suddenly popped it shut. "This is a good time for you to start learning Latin," he said. "You're going on ten years old, aren't you?"

"Yes sir."

"Fine." He left, and I heard him go upstairs and open a closet door and then a trunk. My mother and grandmother and grandfather sat at a smaller table by the stove, all of them looking at me. Julia, my sister, was in bed asleep. She was five years old.

About a week later it was Christmas. I slept soundly the night before, tired from having chased a good three miles after one of the steers which had broken out of the lower pasture.

"Wake up, wake up. Look. Come on. There are *two*."

I turned the light on. It was Julia, standing by my bed; short and chubby, she was barely visible when I was lying down. She was dressed in yellow union pajamas. Her yellow hair shone under the bare light; her round face was white with excitement. "There are *two*," she shouted again. She ran out of the room and down the stairs.

I dressed before I went down. Soon it would be time for me to go to milk. I went down to the living room.

Beneath the red stockings we had pinned to the mantle, there were a bicycle and a tall tricycle. The bicycle was blue and tubular. As soon as I saw it, I began to cry, bawling aloud. "I'm sorry, I'm sorry," I said. "I'm sorry."

"Don't cry." Julia stood before me, tears running on her white cheeks. Her pajamas were stained where she had wet herself.

CHAPTER

9

THEN ONE DAY in a midspring—wasn't I about twelve years old then?—my father came home early. I had just come from school myself, and was dressing in my denim to go out to the fields when he came into the house. At least, I was cocky enough to be twelve years old.

"Home early today, huh?" I asked.

"Yes."

"Couldn't you teach them anything?"

He too was dressing for work in the tan coveralls which made him look so large and solid and strong. He thrust his left leg through the outfit and his left foot searched—almost autonomously, it appeared—for the heavy, high-topped brogan. How huge and stiff these shoes seemed to me. The laces were thick leather thongs which the lower unmetaled eyes would barely admit, but at the top of the shoe the thongs merely crossed about stubby hooks.

"Perhaps not," he said. He was then teaching high school north on Dove River in a tiny hamlet called Jacob. My mother taught there too, and every morning they drove off early to work. The river ran by the road all the way so that they were never out of the fog. I usually didn't see them from six in the morning until about five o'clock in the afternoon. In the kitchen I took a firm apple from the drainboard of the sink and started to leave.

His voice cut through my whistling. "Just you wait a minute," he said. "I'll go out with you. When were you in a hurry to go to work?"

I rubbed the apple on the sleeve of my faded Roy Rogers sweater and he came through the door, zipping up the front of his coveralls. He took his stained hat off the peg in the hall and we went out together.

My grandmother and grandfather were already in the cleared corner of the pasture. He was standing with crutch and cane widely splayed; she was bent over in the long rectangle. Then she straightened and tossed a stone into the road in front of us. By my grandfather's crutch lay a roll of white cloth, plaited in thick strands.

My father called to them. "Have you-all got the broom rake out here?"

"It's right over here," said my grandfather. "Bring one of them poles up as you come. They're layin right in the ditch there."

The poles were about fifteen feet long. They were pine, loose patches of bark stuck on them like scabs.

"Grab the other end and throw it over the fence," said my father.

I went down to the light end and lifted it to my waist. Then the end dropped to the ground, and I was holding two pieces of the rotten bark. My father's jaw became square, and he stretched his right arm forward for leverage and tossed the long pole over the fence. It throbbed violently when it struck the ground. That was the first inkling I had that he was angry.

"Get on through," he said. "Get on."

We took the pole on and dropped it at my grandfather's feet. He eyed my father. "Aint you home kind of early?" he asked.

"Some early, maybe."

"Where's Cory?"

"Your daughter's still teaching school," my father said. "I'll go and get her after a while."

"Why, I'd of thought she would of come home with you."

"She'll be here after a while. I'll go and get her."

He started back after another pole and I had to run to catch up because he was walking so fast.

In about an hour the tobacco bed was finished except for covering it. All the clods and stones were gone from the patch of ground, and the soil had been raked and raked until was almost like baking flour. Even my father's smooth footprints had been erased from where he had tramped in the bed, his arm moving in a steady arc like a windshield wiper as he broadcast the seed.

He looked at the plant bed, his eyes narrowed from the smoke of the cigarette he had rolled until they were almost closed. "That ought to hold until the dogs dig it up," he told us. He picked up the length of canvas and began to unplait it. His large hands fumbled blindly in the cloth.

A dark blue car stopped in the road by the place where the pine poles had lain. My mother was looking anxiously through the car window. The driver was a white-haired man who wore glasses. I had never seen him before.

She rolled down the window. "David, David," she called.

"You see me," my father said.

"Well then," she said. "Yes." She turned and said something to the driver, then she got out of the car, and struggled through the fence somehow without tearing her clothes. It seemed strange because she was wearing her good dress clothes out here. She came straight to my father and stared up into his face. His eyes were still narrowed.

84

"You ought to have told me," she said. "I didn't know anything about it until after school was out. Why didn't you tell me?"

My father turned to me. "Do you know what a paramecium is?"

"Not exactly," I said.

"I'll tell you what I did. I took some moldy alfalfa to school and put it in a jar of water and set the jar in the window sill. That was about a week ago. Yesterday I put some of that water under a microscope and showed my students what a paramecium looked like. It's a tiny little animal."

We were all watching him. He turned to my grandfather and spoke to him now. "Today some jackleg preacher and four or five holy old biddies came down and came in my classroom and told me I was headed straight headfirst into hellfire. They said no man could create life; they told me I was going against the word of the Lord."

"Psh, psh." My grandfather made a hushing noise with his pursed lips. "That don't make no kind of sense to me," he said. "It looks to me like any feller could put a wad of alfalfa in a glass of water."

My father seemed less angry now. He dropped his cigarette and rubbed it out with the toe of his heavy shoe. "I thought I could reply to that. So I said, 'Well, let's go see the principal here. If he thinks that I'm talking against the Bible, he'll be sure to straighten me out.' So then we went to see old Harkins, and what he told me—while they were still standing there—was that somebody in my position had to be very careful. 'You have to be mighty careful,' was what he told me, 'because our young folks here are mighty impressionable about what they see and hear.'" He was mimicking the accent and vocabulary of the speech of a person I had never heard.

"Well, if you'll just talk to him—" my mother began.

He went on. "I think that this is one time that some-one like him should stand up for one of his teachers."

She was very excited. "David, I think he sees your side of it—I really do. He's out here in the car. He brought me home and said he'd be glad to try to get it straightened out with you."

"Just tell him that I don't think he has the guts of a weasel."

She stared at him a long moment, and then turned to go back to the car.

"Wait a minute," he said. "There's no use making the grandfolks walk all the way home. He can give them a ride in his car."

After they had driven off he said to me, "We'd better get this bed covered. A bushel of weed seed has blown into it while we've been standing here talking."

I picked up the opposite end of the canvas and began to untie it. "Are you just going to work around here now?" I asked.

"No," he said. "I'll have a new job inside of two weeks."

We worked for a while in silence. "Can you really create life?" I asked.

"You're here, aren't you?" He leaned and gathered a handful of soil from the plant bed and let it all sift through his fingers. "You come back to this bed in about a month," he said, "and I'll show you some life."

The next day we both went down to see the man Virgil Campbell, who owned the grocery store beside the bridge. Under the bridge, Trivet's Creek, which ran

86

through our farm, poured into Dove River. His store was covered with shingle siding made to look as if it were red brick. We were too early. It was about nine o'clock, and there sat Virgil Campbell holding in his spread arms an imaginary rifle. "Bang!" he said. "Bang, bang!" he cried. He didn't look at us.

"Goddamn," he said. "Three ducks. I got me three ducks already." He didn't turn his head away from looking at the sky.

"Are you all right?" my father asked.

"Well, goddamn," he said. "There's Davy. How you doin, Davy?"

"Are you all right?"

"Don't worry about me." He laid the invisible rifle across his knees. "What you lookin for?" he asked.

"Are you going to open the store any time soon?" my father asked.

He stood up and jangled a good while among his keys. Finally he got the door open. He was very drunk. It seemed queer for my father to let me see what my mother wouldn't even let him mention at the supper table.

We went through the store, passing under the hairy hams suspended from the ceiling, and the sticky peppermint drops lumpy behind the glass cases. When we passed an open case, Mr. Campbell leaned and recovered and put two chocolate-covered mint candies into my hands without saying a word. We went back to sit around the cold stove. The window in the belly of the stove was isinglass; the legs were dappled with spat tobacco juice.

He settled soddenly in a chair and peered at my father. "What're you lookin for, Davy?" he asked.

"I think I'm looking for a job," my father said. "They fired me yesterday, up at Jacob."

"How come?"

"No really good reason. You can find out about it if you want to."

"I'll find out about it whether I want to or not," said Mr. Campbell. "That's how it is, workin in this store here." He was bald, except for a fringe of completely white hair about the back of his head. His face was red; his nose was scarlet with prominent blue veins, a big nose. He scratched his chin. He was slight, but he had a baggy belly. White stubble had sprouted on his chin.

He smoked a cigarette almost halfway down, waiting. "Well," he said, "you married Cory. I'd give the world for Cory. You're all right." He smoked. Finally: "You come to the right man. I'm on the board for the town. They have to listen to me when I talk because I never ask for nothin. I never push nothin on them. You know, I don't even go to the meetins. I aint been to one in three years and they have one every month." He leaned forward in his chair. "You know, they don't like me on that board because they think I don't know nothin. I never finished school or nothin, you know. But one thing they do know is, I can get people to vote."

"You've got a customer," my father said. "That lady there."

Mr. Campbell went forward to sell ten pounds of flour and a gallon of kerosene. He pumped the oil out of a green barrel behind the front door.

Coming back toward us, he said, "Listen. Listen, I can get you what you want. You can just take this job as principal out at Cornhill Grammar School. That man that was out there just quit us. You know that? That board don't know nothin. You'll get more money." He scratched between his legs. "You should've come down to see me the first time you wanted a job."

"O.k.," said my father. "O.k. It takes a while to find out."

88

"You ought to just see how them board fellers are," he said. "They think because I run this little old country store out here in the sticks, or because I drink straight out of the bottle and don't hide it from the preacher, that I aint got the sense the Lord gave a billygoat. But it's the truth I've been in it longer than any of them; I know more about the town and the schools and all the rest of it than all them put together. I can call I reckon almost every man in this town by his given name. If I ask a feller to vote for something he'll do it if he can. None of them can say that. They owe me a whole lot; I don't owe them nothin."

"I can see that," my father said. "What I don't understand is why you don't put on your Sunday clothes and go into politics around here."

"Hell, no," he said, "not me. By God, when I feel like goin huntin, I go. I lock up the store and leave. It don't hurt. Nobody's in that much of a hurry for lard. If I want a drink I take it. Nobody can say anything. You get in politics, people think they've got somethin on you when you do like that."

My father smiled. "The people I know," he said, "think that they already have enough on you, just your being in politics. It's an honor people are happy to hold against you, maybe like being the best possum hunter in the county. They don't mind owning up to the fact that you might be the best possum hunter, because they know they can say too, Who in hell wants a possum."

Mr. Campbell laughed, throwing his mouth open and his smooth head back, showing us the black crowns of his teeth. He pinched his own knee appreciatively. "That hits it, that hits it," he said. He rubbed his nose, and leaned forward to my father. "Come on in the storeroom a minute," he said conspiratorially. "We'll have us a look at something and sign up the trade."

"It's a little early for me," my father said. "It hasn't been very long since I finished breakfast."

"Come on," said Mr. Campbell. "It aint never been that early." He took my father by the arm, and they went into a small back room. Before he closed the door, Mr. Campbell winked at me, and said, "Now, you look after the store for me while we're gone. Don't let nobody run off with that peppermint candy."

They were gone about ten minutes. I watched the fly-specked electric clock that hung over the dry-goods counter. Then they came back, my father rubbing his mouth with the back of his big raw wrist. Mr. Campbell was still laughing.

"We'd better get on back, the boy and I," my father said. "I appreciate what you've done for me, Virgil. I appreciate your talking to me like this."

Mr. Campbell scratched under his arm. "Well, that's all right, Davy," he said. "You'll make us a good man out there. Me and you'll have to go duck huntin together sometime."

"That sounds fine," said my father. They both stood quiet a few seconds, looking at each other and waiting. At last my father spoke. "What I suppose you're going to hear is that I said that man is descended from the monkeys. Something like that, anyway."

"Hell, I knew that," Mr. Campbell said. "Any damn fool can see that."

We walked back up the dirt road that led to the farm. The early mist that had been rising off the river was tearing away. In a locust tree beside the road I saw a bird rooting at something hidden in the loose bark. I slapped my arms against my sides as I walked.

"There's a good man," my father said, "and he's a

man you can learn something from, that is, if you ever learn to keep your eyes open and can learn anything at all."

"What's that?" I asked.

"Independence," he said. "Or, really, the feeling of independence. That's what keeps him happy. I don't think he tries to fool himself that he really is independent—I'm sure that no man who runs a grocery store and has to rely on the good will of his neighbors to sell or to get paid for what he's already sold on credit is really going to believe that he's a completely independent person. But Mr. Campbell has allowed himself enough freedom with his life that he can look independent, anyway; and I suppose that's what is important to him. Seeing that he pretended to be much drunker than he really was when we first saw him this morning, I would say that he *is* concerned about the looks of it. I think the fact is, the more independent you can make the other man believe you are, the more the other man is going to believe that *he* needs *you*."

"Do you need Mr. Campbell?" I asked. I wasn't certain what my father was talking about.

"Don't be silly," he said. "Of course I do. . . . But it's not the same kind of need I'd have for old Harkins if I went back to teach under him after what has happened about that damn little jar of alfalfa. That's what your mother wanted—for me to go back. That's what your mother is like: she wants peace at any price; she wouldn't mind my backing down, she'd rather have me tuck my tail up and jump in a rabbit hole than raise any kind of disturbance. Well, that's o.k., she's a good woman, and I suppose that's the sort of thing women are for. But a man can't choose that sort of thing and feel right about it. At least, I don't want to know the man that can."

"What man?"

He went on as if I hadn't spoken. "Well, anyway, you've seen me make a choice. I don't expect it to make any difference to you if and when you come across a choice like it, but at least you saw me make it."

I said, "Yes sir," but I wanted to say, "Maybe Mother doesn't know what backing down is all about." I didn't say it, because although it sounded like a right answer I didn't understand it. I didn't even understand the question.

"Step it up," he said, lengthening his stride. "We can get a good two hours' work in before dinner."

"Son, what are the two books of the Old Testament that mention the devil?" my grandmother asked.

I looked up from my scribbling. I had got the epic of the Ironbird to a crucial section. The poem was divided into Galaxies, subdivided into Constellations, then into Sectors. I had just come to Galaxy One, Constellation Three, Sector Two, where the Ironbird foresees that the great Golden City of the year 10,000 will die in the flames of war because a secret cannibalistic cult had sprung up in its underworld, an evil sect which sacrificed children.

"I don't know," I said.

"Now, you ought to know that," she said, gazing at me earnestly.

I waited a respectable length of time. "No mam. I can't remember."

"Why," she said, "the book of Job and the book of Daniel. You'll want to remember that, now."

"Yes, mam." . . . *O gleaming Golden City thy streets shalt be ruined,* I wrote.

CHAPTER

10

BACK THEN it was a time when everything was yet
to happen. For although everything did happen, was
already happening in my sight, I did not realize it.
Everything seemed frozen, immobile, statuelike; and
happening was only a shadow which colored in passing
the impassive forms of everyone and everything I knew.
Only that pine-slatted wall in the earlier bedroom truly
showed any change. I could thrust my imagination
against a long lick of the red grain and it would change
from the blade of an Arabian scimitar to the long
finger and pointed fingernail of a witch to a vein of
red gold I had just now discovered in a disused shaft.
But real event—or what I thought of as real event—
would not yield, although my mind hammered at it
time and time again. There lay my grandfather in the
purple casket, the life gone from mouth and face like
water from a bathtub with the plug pulled. His skin
was white under the careful rouge; the creases that emo-
tion had graven on his face were almost full; his eyes
were closed, shades pulled in an empty house. The
sickly smell of the red and white wreaths dizzied me.
I stared intently before they led me away from the
heavy box, but his face remained as motionless as if it
had been painted. When I looked up, the line of
pained and tearful faces seemed frozen too, locked in
the unbreakable instant in which I saw them. *Click,*

click. It was as if I were always taking photographs three feet away, my father's face was square, his full eyes smeary with grief and—it seemed—a kind of longing. *Click.* There was his face, about six inches away, filled with an unreadable expression. *Click.* He was speaking then. "James, you know that I . . . that he. . . ." *Click.* My sister's face turned up to mine, her eyes—she had my father's large eyes—filled with trust, forcing me to remember that I was her older brother. "Isn't everything all right?" she asked. "Mr. Seabury" —the minister—"said everything was all right." She began to cry. She was seven or eight or nine or ten years old. *Click.* My mother's worn, thin hand rode my shoulder like a trained dove. Her skin was fair and thin, blue veins running on the back of her hand. Her tiny gold wedding ring looked like a yellow string tied about her finger. *Click, click.* Like those images which float up and expand before my eyes after long drinking, these pictures were fixed and impassable. Yet, like a wild card in a poker hand or a zero or a decimal stuffed into a row of numbers, all values changed if any one of these images dropped into the cold pool of my thinking. Suddenly it was all charged with terror or envy or love or pity, and I realize now that although it seemed to me that during all that former time I was racing around everything at some impossible super-speed, making all happening appear to be a stopped object, I was actually moving at the same speed as every-one else and that what occurred touched me too. We were all on the same train together. And it was my will to escape or my appetite for comfort which pricked me into believing that some special mode of getting by protected me from the lurching blows of the thick world. I am trying to think about it passionately, try-ing, as Wordsworth claimed to try, to pump myself

94

up again with the voluptuous gas of the memory of things until I am full of the immediacy of the past, which immediacy will give me precision or at least something near correctness; but all I get is *click, click, click, click.* So that the worst I can believe is that in all my past there was no immediacy even in the present moments, that I was always insulated by my peculiarly cultivated temperament from what went on around me, that I was the toad in the garden of what my family— or my sister at least, since only she is near me who would know that place and time—might call Eden. The best that I can believe about me is that I must have detested myself even then. Is there something sexual in this affair between my present life and my past life? I begin to be certain that there is, else I could not stare at it so fascinatedly, like poking shit with a stick. Who was it I wanted to take to bed? Not my mother, as the mind people would say; not my father, not my sister. Not anyone. The truth is that I want to fight back at my past life, the way one dreams of standing up to the bully he used to run away from, and lick it and not have soon again to think that it might trouble my present life. That this return match is not really possible is quite irrelevant: the crux of the matter is, What would happen if I could have a chance to accost, to speak to, and finally perhaps to feel comfortable with my old life, with or without a battle? I would master it, I say; that's what I like to think. *Take yourself up,* I once wrote. But I am certain (and I am trying with my whole strength to kill self-pity) that my past life would master me, would grasp me up and shake me, like a dog shaking a rag doll. My memory of former days is a wound which can in a moment make itself known by uncorking a rotten stink. Like Philoctetes, I must cherish my wound; like Actaeon, my

95

bad memories tear at me, first ripping away the beast's skin within which I have hidden myself. Yet he who snatches away my disguise snatches me too, for I am bound to my mask with a bloody glue; to ask for a sincere answer from me is to tear out my tongue, and, in fact, I no longer understand what the word "sincere" means. My friends expect me to link the word "true" to the word "sincere," or really to stuff the meaning of the latter word into the meaning of the former. But I can tell the truth without being sincere, and I can tell a sincere lie. I have no attitude toward the truth, and I do not like its attitude toward me: for I do know what the truth is—I feel its dark hostility muscle against me. When they led me by the arm away from the heavy casket, the line of sad faces looked like a string of identical beads and my new black shoes pinched my small toes, a sensation almost like being burned with a match. That is what truth is. And after I was taken from the formal procession around the corpse in the sun parlor of the old-new brick house, I went into the kitchen and ate cold fried chicken and drank iced tea. Then I went upstairs to my room and read in *The War of the Worlds* until my father came up to tell me that it was time to go to church to the funeral. That is what truth is. They lowered my grandfather in his coffin into the grave, the canvas straps throbbing with tension as they rubbed the edge of the square hole. To say that I went to his grave in early February, in the sign of Aquarius— airy dry barren masculine—and laid a wreath of wax lilies on his grave would be untrue, but it would be sincere. By God, sincere—as much so as if a prophet divined it out of my opened guts. So, of course, sincerity is even more irrelevant than the truth, for they put him in the ground and shut the ground back and now he is but poor, injured bones clothed in the rich, rotten silk

96

that lined his coffin. His eyes are empty as shotgun muzzles, his skull bears no mark of the emperor. My mind casts itself among his white bones and finds itself rejected. I think of the sweating Negro who drives the power grass mower over his grave, spewing a green spray of damp grass like a shadow beside him. With this man whom I have never met my mind makes acquaintance, for here is meat and breath and, if not purpose, at least motion. If some black tide in the earth thrust up my grandfather, I should not speak to him. We should have nothing to say, fancy staring speechless at bald fact. It was his life which robed his bones, it was his manners that I knew: when these are gone we are strangers. Shakespeare's Pericles found that the sea gave up to him his father's armor, a useful and living object; but had his father the man been cast up to confront him, he would still have been darkling and friendless. *Click, click, click:* like cards dealt to me face up, like turning pages in *Life* magazine, I stare at the pictures in my memory and they stare insolently back: the yellow road clouded with dust and pollen in the August heat, the worn leather shoe tongue my grandfather had made into a fly swat, the clay stain that remained on the preacher's hand when he dropped the earth on the coffin, the sentences of small print that my father brought me away from to go to the church to the funeral: "And beyond, over the blue hills that rise southward of the river, the glittering Martians went to and fro, calmly and methodically spreading their poison cloud over this patch of country and then over that. . . ." One picture does not attract another; they have no sequence other than an accidental one; they tell no story. There is no story to tell. He was laid in a box: the box was buried: this morning I saw a new row of tiger lilies in our neighbor's garden: Missy my daughter

97

has begun to cut her milk molars: the plates for a new book from Winton Press on tobacco plant diseases will cost about three hundred fifty dollars. There is no story to tell, there is only a story to look for.

CARTHAGO SARTAGO. The second time with Judy in her dank bed, spastic in the black grip of lust, thrashing and sweating in the sprung net of sex. Her fat is sticky and oppressive, her hair wet at the roots. The bed makes too much noise; I'm sure that we will wake everyone in the house: her mother, her two kids, and Mavis. It's like driving an empty dump truck over a jolting road. Finally it's over and we lie apart, gasping exhaustedly. She lays her hand inside my thigh; it is like nothing so much as a shaved dog. How disappointing adultery is. It doesn't feel like a sin; it feels like a punishment. The mattress slopes toward her weight, so that I lie with my left arm outstretched in order not to roll to her. Here is this hulk, her body. A pile of useless lumber, warped with sexuality. I see nothing, a void. I may as well be blind.

"Jimmy," she says, "you're real nice. You know?"

"You're nice too," I say absently.

She looses a whispered giggle. "Wasn't that real funny that first night?" she asks. "You remember how Preacher thought it was him I liked all the time? And all the time it was you. I can still see his face." Pause of reminiscence. "I sure do like you."

"Why?"

"You're so nice. You're always so quiet."

"I'm not quiet."

"Yes you are. You never do hardly say anything. But

I can tell about you, you're always thinking about something. I can tell by your eyes, you have real nice eyes." Through her nose, the giggle again. "I can still see his face when I told him he had to sleep on the couch, but you were goin to get to sleep in the bed. You remember how he tried to honey up Mavis then, but she didn't want nothin to do with him. She liked you too. She's real jealous of me now, she won't hardly open her mouth to me. I can still see his face."

Like holding ice in your mouth until it melts, I have the impulse to speak but keep silent and let it die away.

"I bet your wife's real nice," she goes on. "What's she like? I'd like to see her sometime. But I mean," she adds hastily, "I wouldn't say nothin to her or anything. I just wonder what she looks like." Her voice is speculative, wistful.

"She's very nice."

"What's her name?"

"Sylvia."

"That's real pretty for a name. What does she look like? I bet she's a blond."

"Yes."

The giggle. "You must just like blonds," she says.

"Maybe you're right." In the darkness the furniture of the bedroom lacks definite outlines, mere vague presences that point to the walls. From somewhere a dim, gray light shows in the window. In front of the window the spindly rocking chair with my clothes folded carefully on the arm. On my side of the bed a night stand holding a lamp, a clock, a copy of *Screen Romances*, a telephone.

The giggle. "I heard you-all goin out leavin the other night," she says. "Old Preacher was cussin to beat the band."

"Look," I say, "don't you ever telephone the house

100

again. Don't ever call back there."

"Well, you didn't need to be so snotty," she says. "I was just goin to ask you about the party."

"What party?"

"It's next Wednesday night," she says. "It's this feller Preacher knows, I forget his name. Chuck Something, maybe. Me and Mavis are both goin. Preacher is goin. I thought maybe you might kind of like to go."

"Just so you don't call my house any more." Next Wednesday. I can't remember. "What day is today?" I ask.

"You sure are funny," she says. "It's Friday today. Are you goin to go to the party?"

"I suppose," I say. Then, "No."

We lie silent a long while. I can see the room much better now and I realize that the gray light in the window is the coming dawn. The fluorescent clock says four twenty-five. Judy is asleep, giving a peculiarly resonant snore. Between rasps, I can hear the muffled breathing of the others asleep in the house, this bedroom door open for comfort. ". . . butter . . ." Someone, I can't tell whether it's Judy's mother or Mavis, utters at long intervals words from a dream. I think of Sylvia, cool and sleeping, her long hand tucked under her cheek, her knees drawn up to her breasts. I think and think of her lying there alone in bed now. Her dark-blond hair is splashed on the pillow. Her face is calm and sad. In only two hours she must be awake, fixing for John and Missy. And here I am in a town fifty miles away, lying in bed with a female I'm certain I don't know, a beast, Appetite personified. I can't endure my want for Sylvia. I fumble on the night stand and light a cigarette, and begin to dial my own telephone number. The match burns out after I have dialed the area code number and I have to light another.

There are seven rings before I hear the chock of the lifted receiver.

"Hello, hello. Who is this?" Her voice sounds small and tinny, but I feel better at hearing it.

"Hello."

I can't answer. I breathe hotly, anticipating.

"Hello," she says again, and then the beginning of a sob is broken off by the dropped receiver.

—Jesus.

Finally I ease out of the rebellious bed and go to my clothes, trying to make no noise. I hold my pants pocket so that the change won't rattle. Shoes in hand, I go to the door and look back before leaving at the damp mass of Judy.

Her boiled eyes are open. "Bye, Jimmy," she says. Her voice is gluey with sleep.

I go on out.

Apex. The town is pale and bleak in the rising light of dawn. The dozen or so trees which march the edge of the main street are still and shrunken. The stoplights haven't come on yet, and I sneak slowly through the intersections, peering down all the streets. A black-and-white police car at one corner, and two groggy cops watch me with little interest. Everything is closed but a single glowing gas station on the edge of the city proper. And then on the open swift road home.

The sign of Gemini holds the sky, the sign of my birth. My birthday has got past unnoticed, thankfully. I'm sure that Sylvia didn't mention it because she didn't want to put up with my stagy despair. Evening Hesperus dies, and in the morning is reborn as Lucifer. The time of Cancer nears, the sign of my grandmother's birth, and at the walls of the skies Sirius snuffles and scratches for admission. The gray road stretches forward up a gentle slope beyond which only the gray sky is visible so that it seems I might travel in the car into the air and into the ether beyond. Time and place and motive are luxated. The days are beginning to get hot.

I don't know what Sylvia will say. Probably she won't say anything. And I wish that I hadn't telephoned her, frightening her. If she knew where I have been, would she forgive? Probably; yes, certainly. But I feel that I stink of semen and sweat, that I'm black with Judy's bed, that her flabby hands have put blue hand-shaped welts on my nakedness.

This was the second time. It's very strange. Anguish is not so painful, not unbearable, but odd. It's all so very strange. I lick my lips, and on them I still taste the salty, yet achingly sweet, flesh of Judy. Like Christian with his pack of sins, or like Aeneas with Anchises, the huge weight of Judy bends me, my face bowed toward the ground, my feet sinking deep.

> *The heavy bear that goes with me,*
> *A manifold honey spread on his face.*

The soured honey of sensation and unrelenting memory . . . When I was very young, perhaps about four years old—and perhaps not—my father kept a brutal ginger-colored ape to eat me. It was to catch and eat me when he pleased. It was named Modred. But now I keep two bloody red apes chained to myself. Named Will and Appetite, these beasts tear and bite me. When my heart is at last eaten away, they will quarrel and fight over my bones.

—This is all a lie.

The house is alive with my family when I get home. Missy is propped in her high chair, vainly digging in her cereal dish with the little spoon. John sits at the kitchenette table, regarding his grits with grave distaste.

I hear Sylvia fluttering about the kitchen.

"Eat your grits," I say.

"Don't taste good," he says. He frowns.

"Eat them all up. They're good for you. They'll make you big and strong."

"I don't want to be big and strong. I want to be little and not-strong."

"No you don't. You want to be big and strong so you can play football and baseball."

"No, I want to be little. I don't want to play football."

"If you don't hurry, they'll get cold. They don't taste very good cold." Like testing hot water with a toe, he dabs his spoon in.

Sylvia has heard me, and comes through the door bringing a cup of coffee. Lightly, "Hello."

"Good morning."

A bright kiss on my cheek. "How are you this morning?"

"Fine."

"Missy, eat your cereal now, don't play with it. Did you sleep at all last night? John, stop that."

"No."

"Then you can go to bed," she says. "I'll make it up for you, nice and fresh. Just as soon as you finish breakfast."

"Please don't bother with that. Please don't."

She smiles undauntedly. "Of course I will. Don't be silly."

The children are at last released from the table. They run outside, greeting the world and the sun. I finish the last of my toast and light a cigarette for my third cup of coffee. Sylvia sits at the table with me. "I'm going to take a bath first," I say. To wash it off, to wash it all away. "Did the morning paper come yet?" I ask idly.

"Oh, I'm sorry," she says. "That's another of my little

economy measures. You never read the paper, you know. You never even look at it usually. I didn't see any reason to keep on carrying it, just for the funnies."

"That's all right," I say, but unaccountably I feel a bit of regret. This morning I would have liked to read the paper. Receiving the newspaper this morning would be almost like receiving a letter, although I don't know why.

While my bath is running I shave. I see in the mirror that I need a haircut too, rather badly. I toss a wash-cloth into the bathwater without looking at it, and undress. When I turn back to the tub, a rose in the water confronts me belligerently. The rose-print washcloth floats in the tub, half submerged. The picture of this flower looks terribly real and angry. It hovers still and silent in the porcelain. I watch it closely, but it doesn't film or melt: a real rose blooming as it should, the water fresh and clean. I stand naked. At last I get into the tub.

A few minutes later Sylvia comes in, "to keep me company," she says. She sits on the black clothes hamper next the tub.

"The mail came," she says, showing me a brown envelope.

"Anything?"

"Just a couple of ads and this. The bank statement."

"Oh."

"I just looked at it," she says. "Three hundred and thirty-two dollars is all that's left. That's all we have." She sighs. "We just had got our savings account started."

"Are you worried? Don't be worried."

"Well, you know how I am." She rubs her eyes with her slender wrists. "I can't help worrying about everything that comes along. It's the way I am."

"Please don't worry. Things are going to turn up pretty soon. I'm not going to take any chances with money, you know that."

"You know—I don't know if you want to talk about this—you *could* go back to work for the press. Mr. Reynolds said that they haven't hired anybody to replace you yet." Mr. Reynolds is the press editor. "I thought when you quit you were looking for a better job. Or one somewhere else, I mean. But you haven't said anything about looking somewhere else. I mean, if you have been looking, you didn't tell me anything."

"No," I say. "I haven't looked anywhere yet. The press job is all right."

She only looks more troubled than ever. "I'll make up the bed now," she says, and goes out.

The plug pulled, the gagging sound of draining water.

I lie naked in the cool sheets. The striped many-colored curtains are soaked with sunlight; they belly out with the breeze in the open window, eager, gay sails to drive my thinking into the sea of sleep. I have brought *The Time Machine* and my college textbook copy of Tacitus to bed, but can't get up interest in either of them. I hear the children's voices outside, jetting up babbling like water in a fountain. I listen for a while. They shout and squeal, agonized and happy. Then I go to sleep.

I wake up at three-thirty. The children are taking their afternoon naps. Sylvia sits in the living room sewing. I make and eat a couple of salami-on-rye sandwiches and drink milk. Then I go back to bed and go to sleep again.

The next time I wake it is all dark. The only thing I can see is Sylvia's face close to mine, huge and luminous in the dimness. She has just asked me something, I don't know what. "No dice," I say, and roll heavily over. Her hand is light and cool on my shoulder. Then asleep again.

This time sunlight is in the curtains again, patched with shadows of mimosa leaves. The tree grows outside the window. The breeze moves the cloth forward and the leaf shapes descend, like mercury in a thermometer. The breeze falls, the curtain dies, the shapes go back up. Sylvia must have removed the other cover; only a single olive sheet covers me. I look about the room, feeling dislocated, placeless. A cheap blond bedroom suite, studded with concave brass knobs. Unironed clothes piled on the chest of drawers: she must have been waiting until I woke up to begin her ironing. Trinkets and bottles on the vanity. The thin, wavy mirror. Three pictures on three walls: Matisse, Klee, Max Ernst, in reproductions which cost two dollars each. Night stand by the bed holding books, my cigarettes, ash tray, and lamp.

All right. I smoke for a while. All right.

Sylvia has laid out new clothes for me, and I put them on and reload all my pockets. Then I go into my study. Books, pulp magazines, letters, manuscript: a grimy tangle. The man who would live in this room lives like a spider. But I have to write a letter. The typewriter lies open, dust filming the keys.

1902 *Winslow St.*
Winton, N.C.
June, 1962

Mr. Arvin Reynolds
Winton College Press
Box 182
College Post Office
Winton, N.C.

Dear Mr. Reynolds:
   Would the Press please send to me, at the above address, an application for a job with the Press? I

107

*am interested in working in the production depart-
ment, where I understand there is an opening.*

Yours truly,
JAMES CHRISTOPHER

Sylvia taps out her knock on the door, two timid raps
some moments apart. She has heard the typewriter.

"Yes."

She shows only her face in the door. "Are you awake
now?"

"Yes. I'll be out in a minute." I type the envelope
and go on out. "Do you have a stamp?" I ask.

"No. We're out. I was looking for one yesterday.
How do you feel?"

"Just fine. How long did I sleep?"

"Since about nine yesterday morning. Over twenty-
four hours." She shakes her head. "I'm not surprised,
though. You hadn't been sleeping in such a long time.
. . . Do you want something to eat? I'll bring your
coffee."

"No. I'm fine. I'm going to mail this letter, and then
I'm going to get a haircut."

"Will you be back for lunch?"

"I don't know," I say. "I hope so."

12

"THAT'S A NEW haircut there, man," Preacher
says.

"Yes."

Troy's Grill. Preacher sits in a booth, beer before
him, cigarette burning in the triangular ash tray. Now
he wears a dark suit, Texas string tie loosely tied. White
cuff links blink at his wrist, his thin jointy hands drumming on the table. No hat covers the tough red hair,
and his Adam's apple is magnified by the yellow booth
light. "Listen to this 'Slow Twist,' " he says. The record
box jangles and booms. Music hath power. "Listen,
man," he says, "sit down. I've got some news for you."

I sit and give the beer sign with my finger, a gesture
like testing the direction of the wind. "What news?"

"Oh, I don't know. Maybe it's not any news at all.
He wouldn't be lookin for a girl. I mean, after all, you
do go to the girls' bathroom, don't you? It wouldn't be
you, then."

"He who?" I ask.

"Jack Davis is who," he says.

Nothing.

"Man," he says, "don't you know, that's Judy's old
man."

"Oh."

"Well, look now. He's lookin for you. He's already
got the word somebody's been goin around with his
wife. They wasn't no gun that would hold him then.

What did you expect? He just walked away; the honcho wasn't goin to shoot him in the back, him a white man just walkin away. What did you expect?"

"I don't know." My beer comes and I pay the bad-toothed waitress. She does not look at Preacher or me, but over our heads, as at a wraith in the air. A scientific gaze.

"Well, he's around. I'm telling you now. You know what to look for."

"No."

"Look. He's out to slice your ass. I'm tryin to make you understand me. I don't know I can talk any plainer."

"I don't see why he cares about it," I say. "I don't understand how he found out. Maybe he's wrong."

"Oh, goddamn," Preach says. "It's his wife. You know he's goin to find out. Hell, the prison camp aint but about five miles out of the Apex town limit. Especially he's goin to find out about a steady thing."

"Why is it steady?"

He shakes his head, thinking how truly simple I am. He is not even thinking about it; by rote: "It's the how that's steady, not the how much."

"What do you mean?"

But he has already given up. Me he can't figure, especially on this point. "That Mavis is all right, man," he says. "That Mavis is a sweet piece. You know it?"

"I didn't know."

"It's the truth," he says. "It's God's truth."

I prepare myself for a wearisomely detailed lie.

"All the time you was there," he says, "she was rubbin her legs against me under the table. I could tell you didn't know nothin about it, she kept smilin at you. But that's how it goes, man. Just as soon as you left to go get your nose powdered, she commenced askin me a

110

lot of questions. You know, do I like to dance, and did I get to see Rory Calhoun in some picture. So we was gettin along fine; the only trouble was she wasn't goin to let me have any that night. Not with you around there, runnin after Judy with your tongue hangin out. But I went back the very next night, and we had one good time, us. It's the truth, man, it's God's truth. Well. The next night after that . . ." And on, and on.

"I can't see it," I say. "The first time I saw her was less than a week ago."

"Can't see what?"

"About her husband George. If he's in prison, I don't see how he could hear about anything. Who told you?"

"Well," he says, "I was just fixin to tell you. It was Mavis told me. It was Judy that told her, but then that Judy, you know her. She didn't want nobody to tell you." He giggles reminiscently. "She just likes to stir up trouble. But I thought if somebody was comin around to slice your ass, you better know about it."

"Well, thanks. I guess. I still can't make any sense of it."

"His name's Jack too, man, not George."

"Jack who?"

"Jesus, man. You better come alive upstairs. You're gettin just plain ridiculous."

Home again. I stand in the doorway to my study, just looking. Odor of dust, of damp closeness, of newsprint, of very old cigarette butts. This dirty little hole makes my flesh crawl. Sylvia sits gingerly in the wicker chair at the ancient desk. She sits almost fearfully, looking at the mess before her.

"Well," I ask, "just how would you go about cleaning it up? It looks impossible to me. Maybe we should just burn the room, and put a new wall in here. Or just wall it up as it is. You know, 'For the love of God,

111

Montresor!' Really."

She shakes her head. "I don't know, James. After you told me not to, I didn't think about it." Another shake of her head, meaning: *Men* . . . "If I'm going to clean it, you'll have to help me," she says. "I won't know what to keep and what to throw away." She disentangles a sheet of the new manuscript. "I'm sure you'll want to keep this," she says.

I cross to her and read over her shoulder. *There is no story to tell, there is only a story to search for.* "I don't know. That stuff is all wrong, I think. I think it's full of lies. Just throw it away. . . . No. Wait . . ."

She holds it apprehensively in both hands.

"Maybe I'd better keep it. No . . . I don't know. We'll be better off if you just clean the room yourself. Just throw everything out."

"No," she says. "You'll need some of these things. You'll just have to help me."

Then we begin. Axe and machete. I decide that I don't want ten-year files of *Doc Savage*, *Weird Tales*, *Amazing Stories*. Even the worthless, costly issues of *Thrill Book* go: twenty-seven fifty each for four issues. Here goes Edgar Rice Burroughs; here goes H. P. Lovecraft. Here goes M. R. James, Ralph Milne Farley, H. Rider Haggard. Goodbye to Tarzan, to Tom Swift, to the Hardy Boys, to Allan Quatermain. "Jesus," I say. "*Tom Swift and His Electric Condom.* Didn't I ever do anything but read when I was a kid? How much time do you have when you're a kid? If I read from now to the end of my life, I couldn't read all these books." But I remember that for kids there is no time at all. A book is only a moment, snatched up and gulped, between one noisy game and the next; or read a sentence at a time, sipped at during the long dreams one dreamed in the apple trees or in the hay loft. Good-

112

bye to Sherlock Holmes; goodbye, *Scaramouche*; goodbye, Jules Verne.

But I will save H. G. Wells. "Here," I say, piling the Wells titles together on the desk. "I *will* keep these, I don't know why."

Sylvia looks at the precarious stack. "He's supposed to be pretty good, isn't he? I mean, literary."

"You've got me. A book is a book. I'm just sick of looking at this other stuff."

Farther into the morass. The first primitive pornography I got at the age of fourteen or fifteen. I traded fifty bubble-gum fighter-airplane cards for this little booklet. The girlie magazines of later adolescence, my hot eyetracks still fuming on the pages.—Sylvia laughs delightedly at one particularly cowlike specimen.—And now the real junk: a badge reading, "I'm a real Pal," ticket stubs to Saturday western movies, a pipe rack that never worked out, an indescribable cylindrical brass object, purpose unknown, a railroad flare, expiration date June, 1943, dead flashlight batteries, parts of an old radio, jumble of rusty fish hooks, pie-slice-shaped chips of 78 rpm records, wire wrapped about a toilet-paper tube (the beginning and the end of a crystal radio set), stubby pencils, clothespins, queer stones, broken package of Home Run cigarettes, Captain Marvel pennant which used to glow in the dark, a card explaining Superman's secret code, plastic toys from boxes of Pep cereal, a rubber handle grip from my blue bicycle, a coverless baseball half melted away, broken slingshot, desiccated remains of a caterpillar cocoon, raccoon's mummified paw, unopenable bottle of model airplane glue, random ruddy stamps dropped from an album, cellophane stickers to attach the stamps to the album pages, two Joker cards and one Jack, an Indian arrowhead my father had turned up plowing in

113

the bottom fields, a few odd chess pieces and checkers, couple of comic books, broken toy pistol, broken water pistol, stringless yoyo, match covers, bottle caps, a filthy clip-on bow tie, empty typewriter ribbon spool, broken fly line reel, thread spools, my grandfather's smaller pocket knife, all blades broken, one argyle sock, six-inch file worn almost smooth, hammer head with nail prongs broken, small screwdriver, initialed cuff links, friction belt buckle, plastic laniard made at summer camp, two brass buttons, arm off one of my sister's dolls, assorted rifle cartridges, empty shotgun shells, torn map of Europe with the boundaries all wrong, batch of knobs, screws, bolts, keys, a rusty bicycle lock, two musty Bibles and a pocket-sized New Testament, my grandmother's yellow thimble. A handful of curled photographs with the scorched look of time on them: my mother and father standing together, he wearing a vest, much skinnier than I ever remember seeing him; my grandmother on the front porch of the big brick house, holding a very young baby, my sister or myself; about twenty persons in caps and gowns, myself to one side in a sailor suit, a mascot to the graduating class where my father was principal; my sister and I on a professional photographer's bench, she with dimples and long yellow curls; my grandfather wearing a wary grin, propped on his sticks.

"I didn't know about this," I say, retrieving a card from the stack poised on the desk above the waste can.

"What is it?" she asks.

"Look. It's a Code of Conduct card, an Army card."

"Your father was in the Army, wasn't he?"

"No. I don't know where it came from. Nobody in my family was ever in the Army. I must have traded something for it."

"Oh," she says, brandishing her already black dust

cloth. "Well."

Only rules one and two have remained stable, it seems. The Korean War. I read rule two: *I will never surrender of my own free will. If in command I will never surrender my men while they still have the means to resist.* How queer it is. How queer to find this rule, for the first time, perfectly understandable. The trouble has been that I did surrender of my own free will. I succumbed in an instant, although there is now no way of locating this instant lost in the interminable row of little boxes which enclose all instants. The real true trouble is that I have been thinking of my will as an enemy, something inimical to my self, something which fights at my self. The ape chained to me, red and vicious. I have been acting as if I had surrendered, but the realization of the act of surrender has never forced itself upon me. To begin again, and to go straight forward and never to surrender: isn't this the purpose of the self? The self a flowery graveyard shooting personality up to withstand and to conquer moment and circumstance, a terrible martial putting-forth. Perhaps, perhaps not: only a very brave metaphor will engender courage in the confronting of event. It's best not to think about it; it's best merely to wait and to rely upon whatever force or habit it is that causes motive to well up in the mind out of the ebon chaos of impulse.

I stand back and breathe heavily and look at the crazy rubble that Sylvia is heaping up to throw away. We both sneeze now and then, the mustiness crowding in upon us. Everything seems as garish and polychrome and illogical as a comic book. The acid of fear begins to shoot through my veins. My head is filled to bursting with white sensation. I am sweating heavily, and the short hair on the back of my neck prickles. "Don't," I say. "Please stop. Don't throw it away."

115

She looks at me. "All right," she says. "It's all right. I knew you didn't really want to."

Something like a watery veil, like heat waves off a hot highway, blurs my vision. "Yes. Yes, I do." It's hard to talk. "I want to get rid of it."

She grasps both my hands, holds them tightly. "Why don't you go lie down?" she asks. "I'll leave everything just like it is now. I have to go see what the children are doing anyway."

"No. No, really. I really do want to get rid of it." The right angles of the corners of the study seem to be growing wider. "I'll go off for a while," I say. "Just throw it all away while I'm gone. Don't keep anything."

"Not even this?" She points to the manuscript. She still hangs to the belief that I was writing a book.

"Nothing. All of it."

I take an aspirin and go out and drive to Troy's Grill again. Preach is still here, sitting quietly and listening.

Come on, let's twist again,
Like we did last summer.

Bare ruined choirs where late. "You're back again," he says. "You aint even wore the new off of your haircut yet." He nods toward the juke box. "I sure do like this song," he says. "They play it all the time, but I don't care. Your wife run you off?"

"No. I just wanted to get out. I'm going back in a few minutes."

He nods wisely. "That's what they all say. They's people set in here five, ten years and said that. They's roots growin out of their ass plumb through the floor. I bet you aint even been home since you left here."

"Maybe they're telling the truth," I say. "Maybe I am too."

116

A condescending glance. "You've done already gone," he says. "I just don't pay you no mind. Did you know when Jack Davis comes lookin for you this here's the first place he's goin to look?"

"Why?"

"Well, this is where you hang out, aint it?"

"I drank my first can of beer in here a month ago. I don't—'hang out'—anywhere. I don't know any of the people you know." I feel very bad. "I don't hang out anywhere," I add heavily.

"Yes you do," he says. "You hang out here, if you didn't but know it. Everybody knows you do. You're here about as much as I am, and I hang out here, don't I?"

"I guess so."

"Trouble with you, man, is you don't keep your eyes open. You got to keep your eyes open and know what's goin on. You don't know what's goin on."

"I know that," I say tiredly. "I'm not sure I want to know what's going on."

He puffs unweariedly at a cigarette, sips his beer. I take a cool pull from my own sulkily brought bottle. "That Jack Davis is goin to come after you," he says. "You want to know that." He leans forward abruptly, his voice lowered. "Listen, man," he says softly, "I've got a good thing goin with that Mavis. She's the sweetest little thing I ever got after. You know?"

"I'll tell you what I know," I say. "You're lying in your teeth. You haven't got near her yet, and it'll take you at least six months to do it. You spend your time letting people know what a cool cat you are, and how fast and how much you make out with women, but you haven't had a girl in a good long time and it'll be a good long time before you have one. You spend all the time you have, endless time, trying to manufacture un-

117

interesting lies. Lies to tell me mostly, but changeable lies to tell to other people who know you better than I do. The truth is, you spend most of your time sitting here trying to think of lies and wishing that you could think of more. The man you happen to be talking to is the man you want to impress. . . . You're right—I don't see what goes on, I don't have my eyes open. But I wasn't born yesterday, either. Do you think I don't know what a woman wants, or what a man wants? Bull shit is bull shit. It always smells and tastes the same. I can look at you hard, and I can look right through you, like a piece of glass. There's nothing in you but a whine and a fart and a lie. What did you think? That you were my teacher, to teach me all about what goes on in the world?"

He grins a thin grin, showing his yellowed teeth. One hand he waves in the air. His shirt cuff is ringed with dirt. "Man," he says, "that bull shit. I wouldn't have knew how it tasted until you told me." He breaks out an irritating laugh, the whole sound coming from his throat.

"I'm not even through talking yet," I say.

He pinches the tip of his bony nose. "Well, man, that's all right," he says, rising from the booth, "but I've got better things to do than sitting around here listenin at you run off at the mouth." He shrugs his shoulders into their nests in the jacket of his suit. Looks about him, as if reconnoitering mined territory. "It aint healthy to be around where you're at, anyway; not with that Jack Davis loose."

"That's all right," I say. "You needn't worry about me. If that's what you're doing instead of just trying to scare me."

"See you around the way, man," he says. He leaves, a cigarette still burning in his ash tray.

118

I put his cigarette out and leave the booth and move to the bar. The heels of my shoes hanging on the highest rung of the bar stool, my elbows propped on my knees, cigarette in my left hand, warm bottle of beer in my right, I sit. Greasy potato chips in cellophane. Huge blue glass globe belted by SCHLITZ rotates slowly over my head. A great pocket watch advertising Budweiser turns and turns. The barkeeper watches me suspiciously, the dim bar light rounded into globules on his horn-rimmed glasses. Seven-Up sign: high school couple, the girl pure cheesecake, skating on an icy pond. Have fun, have Seven. I keep on drinking. Barkeeper carefully inserts a tooth pick into the left corner of his mouth. How goddamn Southern this place is. Sound leaking out of the juke box like an oily, flooded ditch. Plastic-covered booths at my back, filled with groups of three and four and five, never two. Not the right kind of place, middle of town. *Ping* of the cash register. Endless thumping of the door to the men's room. I ought to call Sylvia. . . . In a while.

The record box makes improbable noises. The scary reversion comes: the gooseneck lamps in the booths are elephant trunks, the beer tap squirts urine. The unending running and drumming and humming of the air conditioner fans in the place. The night outside is hot, the stars teary in the sky. All the neon is shrouded with its own glowing ghost. I reach for a cigarette before I realize that one is already burning in my hand. What can you do? I don't know what to expect. Isn't what I told Preacher the truth? Yes. Yes, yes. Say, Yes. *I will never surrender of my own free will.*

I get up to go to the bathroom. A line of sideburned boys, all tattooed, all leaning against the wall as patiently as if they were dead, stuffed corpses propped up to deceive me.

119

But my hair gets zipped in my zipper. Oo—carefully —o.k. The lavatory. A strange bad face glares at me from the window in the towel roller. A face like an empty wallet, meaty and insensible. Very slightly curly hair flattening into pencil-like strands. Full, colorless lips. The face of a woman.—I should have had my sister's face. I should have gone into the Army. First Lieutenant James Christopher. I should have been an architect, a physicist, an expert in interstellar googol-plexes. . . . I should have gone home a while ago.

I don't go home, though. I don't like to go home drunk and guilty. Where does that get you? It never got me anything but comfort from Sylvia. Comfort and understanding, so that pretty soon I felt twice as guilty as before.

I stand at the back of the house, whacking at the screen door. The homogenized kitchen light shows cold and bare through the black screen, and then the large rectangular form of my sister smashes a black hole in the light of the doorway.

"Who is it?"

"Me," I say.

"All right." She comes and unlatches the screen. "Come on in, James. James, I hope you know what time it is." The bathrobe she is wearing makes her look large and solid with the light behind her, and with the shoulders puffed like that, like epaulettes, she seems very masculine. First Lieutenant Julia Christopher.

"I never think about that," I say.

"You ought to, then," she says. "It's twelve-thirty. I hope you didn't come here at this hour on purpose to worry Sylvia."

"Oh, for Christ's sake. I just came after coffee."

120

"Well. You're in a pleasant mood, I see. Are you drunk?"

"Some drunk," I say. "I never think about that either."

She precedes me into the kitchen and places a kettle of water on the stove. She places a saucer and an empty cup before me on the small kitchen table. She spoons a thick black powder into the cup. "Instant," she says.

"I see."

She leans against the wall, waiting; I sit at the table, waiting. "I know you think that I'm always into your affairs, and that I'm always nagging at you, but it does seem to me you ought to show a little more consideration for Sylvia." She gets a package of cigarettes off the gas range and takes one out. "And there are the children, too."

I stare at an arrangement of cute trivets on the wall over the stove. "For Christ's sake": a little wearily now.

She blows the smoke straight toward me. "You're certainly in a good mood. Who bit you?"

"I don't know. I'm just p.o.ed. I've been wanting to tell this guy off, and finally I did. Tonight, I mean. But I didn't get it all out, there was more I wanted to say and I didn't get a chance. I feel sort of unfinished, if you know what I mean."

"Well," she asks, "did you come over to take it out on me?"

"Yes. Yes, I did. Do you remember about my asking you how you got to be older than me? I want to know how you got to be bigger and stronger too. The only reason, real reason, I want to know is because I don't believe you did. I believe I'm stronger and you backed down and now you're faking me out."

"You think I lie to you."

Thin *thweep* of the kettle boiling. She takes it off the

121

stove very quickly; I see that she doesn't want to wake her sleeping husband or the kids. She pours the water into the cup and it rises black, foaming and steaming.

"No, I could find out a lie before now. I think you're just faking me out."

"I don't know what you're trying to say."

"I'm not trying, goddamnit, I *am* saying. I used to protect you. You were smaller than me, my little sister. And then somehow you got the notion you were protecting me, and some way you got me to believe it. That's what I mean."

"Well," she says, "it's true. You've always had women —if it's the woman part of what you're saying that bothers you—to protect you. Sylvia—"

"There," I say. "Right there. That sentence sounds just like Daddy."

She hasn't even heard me. "Sylvia protects you, she doesn't let a thing get to you that you don't want her to. I'm doing my share too. You just resent it because I'm trying to get you to come out of it a little. Mother protected you when we were children; then, she was always standing by."

"No," I say. "If that's what you think, you're flatly wrong. What did she have to protect me from?"

"Daddy."

"He wouldn't have hurt me. He wouldn't ever have hurt me."

"No, of course not. But there was something about him that disturbed you. It literally tore you up, whatever. It was that that she was standing by for."

"You're wrong about everything, especially right now. I protect Sylvia, that's what I'm for. I protect you, too. I'm protecting you right now."

She's smiling now, thinking that we've passed the bad spot. "How are you protecting me now?"

122

"I'm holding it in," I say. "If I let my brain explode right now, it would blow the house out of the city."

"That's terribly melodramatic."

"So what?"

13

THE BIG BRICK HOUSE had more people in it
now than at any time since I had lived there with my
grandparents, but now it was more hushed than ever.
Downstairs my grandfather lay dying. He lay on his
back in the north bedroom, the bedroom in which I
had started the fire some years ago. He had built the
house again to his—at last, everyone sighed—satisfac-
tion only last year, and now he had, they said, only
days to live, weeks at the most.

Much had been salvaged from the burned house: all
the walls were still intact, and some of the furniture
had been saved, and some of the fixtures. For instance,
the same heavy hickory banister ran up the new stairs
that had run up the old. The same four-legged bathtub
still stood in the bathroom. Even the old pendulum
clock now rested on a new mantel. But many things
were gone: the woolen picture of a camel rider in Jeru-
salem which used to hang on the north bedroom wall,
the autographed picture of Franklin D. Roosevelt,
the marble-top chessboard my grandfather had made,
all my grandmother's dresses (she was still making new
ones). The old Silvertone radio had been replaced by
a television set which no one ever watched. In fact,
until about a week ago the life which the old house
had contained still drove forward, almost as if it had
never stopped. But the burned smell, an odor like the
odor of wet ashes, remained in the house, pervasive as

air. Nothing would quite kill it: not the bottles of medicine that glittered in the room where my grandfather lay, not the piles of flowers that were sent him, not even the banks of wreaths that later surrounded his coffin.

I sat upstairs in the same room where I had lived before. The walls were still made of pine slatting, but these walls had been painted white, so that only a faint impression of the streaked grain came through. I could instill no life into these walls no matter how hard I stared; they still remained the same: blank, accusatory. It was mid-August, sweltering hot in my room under the asbestos shingles. In the afternoon, from about four o'clock, the westward sun burst heavily into my room. Dust motes crawled upward in the shaft of light. When the westward moon was full, the windows ached with its light, and the white walls seemed very close around me. Here were the cheap magazines and books, the two great beds, the black desk with my grandmother's notes to me dangling from the corner.

There were six rooms in the upstairs. At the north end of the house, directly above the bedroom where my grandfather lay, a room entirely disused. A single coverless cot in one corner, several trunks filled with letters, bank statements, old trinkets, blankets. A stack of old housekeeping magazines with advertisements like "She saved two cents but spoiled the dinner," and pictures of the gremlins wrecking the war effort. Two large windows faced across our fields toward the gray mass of Chambers Mountain; its lower slopes were quilted with oak woods, the top splotched with great grassy balds. The summer rains came out of the north. Standing at these windows I could watch the sky coagulate about the mountain summit and the webbed veil of the rain descend. Opening the window, I would find the air electric with hush, suddenly cool. Next this room was a tiny bathroom; the toilet didn't work because the drain had never been properly set up. At the south end of the house, another bedroom. Two feather beds sat on each side of the door, the walls were pine slatting painted white, as in my bedroom; a large desk, a large trunk, a black vanity with five mirrors which could be set at angles except for the middle one, which was fixed; again, two large windows which looked southward, but here the view was blocked by a two-story wooden shed across from the house. Under these windows, however, ran the electric power lines for the house. I could draw a heavy platform rocker to these windows and sit to practice smoking cigarettes and to watch the sparrows which alighted on the lines puff and flirt and chatter. A small door in the left wall of this bedroom opened into a very small dusty attic. The attic was so small that I had to remain half-bent whenever I went in: here was nothing but a couple of small trunks filled with old newspapers, an old sausage mill, last year's (and next year's) tobacco bed canvas hung from the ceiling out of the reach of mice, about two dozen empty canning jars. The attic was about four feet wide and four and a half feet deep. A single window in the south end showed only the wooden shed. Directly opposite my own room was a small room of no discernible use. Two gabled windows faced the sunrise and the grapevine which ran on the hog-wire fence behind the house. This room was empty except for eight or ten pictures in heavy gilt frames. These must have been daguerreotypes: they showed the parents and grandparents of my own grandparents, and some of my uncles and aunts in their earliest youths. The men had mustaches sharp as knives, great glassy chins, direct, forbidding eyes. The women who stood beside them

126

had gross-featured mannish faces, their hair braided over the tops of their heads. My uncles looked in the pictures nearly the same as they did now, but diminished. One of them, standing by an axe on a chopping block and dressed in what looked like a long nightshirt, had borne the name they gave me. He had died at the age of nine, his blood poisoned, a victim like my grandfather of the bad country medicine of forty years ago.

The house was very quiet, but as I read or idled in my scorching bedroom I could hear cars stopping often outside the house, the doors thumping solidly. At times I could hear from the kitchen below the rising murmurs of my grandmother's or my parents' voices as they greeted someone they had not seen in a very long time, someone they had perhaps never expected to see. It was like an occasional flare of static on the radio. Now and then I would slip out the window and go to lie on my belly with my head hung upside down over the eaves. In this position I could see the dining room part of the kitchen, and often the head and shoulders of some country stranger come to pay his respects. I ate better now than I ever had before. My mother and grandmother were always at the new electric stove, both of them bright in new long aprons. My grandmother was very hesitant about the new stove, and she was always licking her finger and touching each of the four eyes on the top of the stove to find if any of them were burning. Even in the yellow August heat the tiny coal stove which fed the hot water jacket was always going, the pipes banging and coughing as the water roiled in the galvanized tank. The kitchen was as hot and steamy as I imagined the planet Venus to be.

Almost everyone who came to visit my grandfather had to be fed. Teamaking and coffeemaking were continual. Some of his acquaintances had to come a long

way, or they worked at odd hours, so that even breakfast foods had to be prepared in quantity. There were
always fried chicken, fresh or cold, boiled corn and
creamed corn, fresh tomatoes, eggs, sausage, ham, cornbread, biscuits, applesauce, okra, mashed or boiled potatoes, white chicken gravy and salty red-eye gravy, rice,
all kinds of cakes and pies, old jars of honey, even cured
venison had been brought out at last. No one noticed
or cared what or how much I ate so long as I didn't
get underfoot or interrupt someone who was talking.

My father kept away from the house as much as he
could, finding tasks in the farthest corners of the farm
where he had never worked before. He didn't ask me to
come help him; he hardly spoke to me. But every afternoon about four o'clock he came back to the house and
ate quickly and talked to whoever had come to visit my
grandfather. Then after a while he and I went out to
milk. He rarely went into the bedroom where my grandfather lay.

I didn't know many of the persons who came: there
seemed an interminable stream of them. Some of them
had known him for a long time, for most of his life;
most of them had known him only after his legs were
shattered and, like myself, they could imagine him no
other way than crippled, his arms towering him up
stilted on his sticks. All kinds of cars and trucks
brought them here, and almost all of them wore creaky
new denim overalls and stiff white shirts. The men
looked red and unbending in their Sunday clothes, the
women quite disarrayed in bright print dresses. Very
few of the visitors were as young as forty years, and
some of them were in their eighties. Dust boiled up
in the road like a long yellow scarf trailing behind their
cars.

When no one was there but him I went into my

grandfather's room. He lay heavily in the center of the bed. The skin on his face was stretched tight, and gray stubble shadowed his cheeks. His eyelids covered the sharp green eyes. His horny hands lay by his sides. He breathed quickly and shallowly. Only a short, rather dirty nightshirt covered him, so that his legs were bare. I saw them swollen, black and purple in patches. I stared. Somewhere in his black right leg inched the clot of blood, aimed, like an already shot but horribly slow bullet, at his heart. His eyes flicked open, but he did not see me, staring blindly up at the ceiling. His eyes closed again, his right hand closed slowly. I went as quietly as possible out of the house and stood in the road behind. If he could have seen me at all, he could have seen me here through his bedroom window. I looked out over the cornfields below. Piled thunderheads threw islands of shadow down upon the fields. In the bays of sunlight the corn looked greasy and dark, almost black. At the tenant house on the other side of the fields Uncle's wife was hanging out washing. A red blanket jerked like a flag in the breeze, some code signal which I couldn't read. Uncle wasn't at the farm now; he had gone to stay with one of his brothers for a while. I had heard him talking to my father. "I'm sorry about it, but I can't help it," he had said. "But I know you aint goin to make me stay around here and watch the old man die. I couldn't stand it to do it. I wouldn't be no help to you nohow." My father had said, "No. You know I'm not going to make you do anything. I'd leave myself if I could, but I can't. At least I don't see how I justly can." A pillar of cloud scudded swiftly overhead and put me in its shadow.

I went back up to my room and wrote more of the epic of the Ironbird. Galaxy Two, Constellation One,

Sector Five. The great golden King of the planet Venus was dying on his throne. Of his three sons, only the youngest had proved superior to fleshly temptation, and to him the King gave his throne, admonishing him to beware any evidence of cannibalistic cults. After a while the storm began, a loud dog-days storm which would drive Hurl under the bed. The odor of ozone from the blue lightning, the thunder breaking with a noise like houses falling. Rain whipped the hills and spattered on the window. A long spout of it leaped out of the end of the eaves gutter. The walnut tree in the yard dipped forward and back, a lonely minuet. Then it stopped. The new breeze cleared the sky, like someone stripping a bed. Everything was clean and cool, and in only a few hours the breeze and sun would dry the muddy roads.

It was almost milking time. When I went downstairs to find my father, everyone was crying and holding one another. My grandfather had died during the storm. "He just opened his mouth," my mother said. Her face was wet. "He was trying to say something." Not words, but his spirit had risen out of his mouth and silently up the air, like invisible cigarette smoke.

I wandered out toward the barns. The cows had come down to the gate of the pasture, but I didn't know whether to turn them into the lot yet. I went into the barn. Sacks of crushed corn lay piled about; a few sacks of cottonseed meal sat by the door. Sunlight streamed as through Venetian blinds through the north wall. Random planks had already been knocked out of the wall, so that air could circulate when the tobacco stalks were hung to cure. I pulled the small wooden cover off the mouth of the feed chute and tugged down and opened a sack of the crushed corn and spilled it down the chute into the bin in the milking room. Then I

130

threw down a few handfuls of cottonseed meal. I didn't want to work, but I didn't want to sit still either. It was very quiet. A barn swallow perched in the wall where a board was missing. I looked about me remembering how a long time ago my sister and I had found the escaped convicts here, huge gray men sitting on the feed sacks. It had been in a January. It had been very cold; I had tried and tried to get Julia to come back to the house out of the cold, but she kept sitting down. Finally my father had come to see about us. The barn had not changed since then, and that had been seven or eight or nine years ago.

I climbed on a pile of the stuffed sacks and lay down. Above me the tier poles stretched like arm bones across the room under the tin roof. I could hear the halting tramp of pigeons on the tin. Only last year Uncle and I had been on the barn roof, painting. I took a cigarette out of the cuff of my pants. I always hid one there, in case I got a chance to practice smoking when I wasn't in the house. I lit it and gagged once and watched the blue smoke mingle in the zinc color of the roof. I began to cry very softly. Someone standing six feet away couldn't have heard me. Through the tears the straight bars of sunlight began to run and to melt into big dollops of yellow light. When I squeezed my eyes tight, these lumps of light rounded into globes and shot out sharp arms all over. This way they looked like incandescent spiders. I squeezed tighter and these shapes shrunk to fuzzy balls which looked as if they were drawn with green ink on tissue paper. Blue and orange haloes rose to encircle these balls.

My father's voice woke me. "Get the hell off," he said. "Hurry. Hurry, damnit." He jerked me off the sacks to the floor and seized the two sacks on the top of the pile and ran out the door and threw them into the road. His face was white and he was breathing hoarsely, his mouth open. I stood dazed as he grabbed two more sacks up and threw them into the road. He came back and inspected the remaining sacks carefully. Closing his mouth, he sniffed deeply, going from one place to another. "I hope to God for your sake that I've got it all," he said. "What the hell do you think you're trying to do? No. You don't think; I was supposed to have learned that five years ago. Are you going to burn up the whole countryside, or will even that satisfy you?"

A brownish commingling of smoke rose from the sacks which lay in the road.

After they brought his body back from the embalmer and laid it among the banked flowers in the sun parlor, all the persons who had come to see him sick came again to see him dead. But now there were more. The family took less notice of me than ever, and I took particular care to keep well out of my father's path. Now he seemed preoccupied, more absent than ever, and his eyes were always red at the rims. I never saw my mother or grandmother. Julia kept asking me to play with her, but I was afraid that it was wrong to.

The people kept going by the coffin like an army going single file along a narrow mountain trail. I kept writing a queer account of it in the poem about the Ironbird. At last a lady whom I had never seen came upstairs to my bedroom and told me to put on my best Sunday-school clothes. We were going to the church in a little while. I washed my face and dressed and went downstairs. I heard my father talking to someone as I came down the steps. "I'm worried about James," he said. His voice was shaky. "He and his

132

granddaddy were together almost every minute of the day for the past . . ." He fell silent when he saw me, and he and the other man stood back against the walls to let me pass between them. I went into the kitchen. "You come this way now, son," said the lady who had told me to dress. She led me into the parlor. The murmuring stopped as I stood in the doorway. All the people turned their faces toward me, blank pearls on a string. The grave lady leaned and whispered in my ear. "Just walk by and look at him and be a big man, now. This is how you'll always want to remember him." I walked forward, dizzy and slightly sick from the arrayed red and white wreaths. His face was smoother than I had ever seen it. It was like a piece of furniture. He looked like a great doll. I looked up at the motionless faces around me, and for an instant they looked almost like my grandfather's. My mother was walking just behind me. "James," she said. "Oh." She put her warm, dry hand on my shoulder. I glanced at her thin wedding ring. Two ladies came and led her away from me, and I went out on the front porch.

Mr. Seabury, the minister, was on the porch, squatting on his heels, talking to my sister. His thin gold-rimmed spectacles were even with the top of her head. She too was newly dressed: a white linen dress with a wide sash, white silk calf-length stockings, black patent leather shoes. Mr. Seabury arose when I came out, and Julia turned to me. Her face was round, her eyes seemed large as eggs. "Mr. Seabury said everything was all right," she said. At first it sounded gay, but then she began to cry. She rubbed her cheek with the back of her hand. "Isn't everything all right?"

I thought that what she meant to ask was, Aren't you my brother? Don't you know about things? "Yes," I said.

Mr. Seabury patted my back. His hand was small and soft. "That's right, James," he said. "You must be brave and teach your little sister to be brave too. You must learn to be a man, now."

"Where's Mama?" she cried. "Where's Daddy?"

He gave her his long white finger. "Here," he said, "we'll go find them."

There was no one in the kitchen. I opened the refrigerator and took out a cold chicken breast. Then I found a glass and poured tea from a wet jug and put a lot of sugar in the glass. I sat at the table, eating with my hands. My father came in. He had been crying, and his face was flushed. His face looked more square than ever with the collar of his new shirt drawn tight and the slender black tie flat against his shirt front. His eyes were red and wet. He stood about six feet away looking at me for a long time. He looked as if he wanted very much to talk to me, but couldn't think where to begin. At last he came and sat in the chair next to me at the table. I put the piece of chicken in my lap. He leaned forward until his face was about six inches from mine. It looked so huge that it was unreadable. "James," he said, "James, you know that I . . ." He stopped and waited a long time. "That he . . . I've tried to teach you about . . ." He leaned back, not looking at me now. All expression was gone from his face, as if it had fallen asleep. He lit a cigarette. Soon they came to take us to the church.

The whole family went to the front pew, where none of us had ever sat. We had always sat toward the back of the church. The coffin and the mounds of flowers stood before us, just inside the railing. Mr. Seabury came to the pulpit and began to talk. He had put a black robe over his dark suit. Behind him, the choir sat motionless. Some of the choir members were my class-

134

mates in high school. I watched them peek at me, their eyes filled with fear.

"This man who was in his life a builder of fine houses has gone to that great Mansion where all souls are received joyfully. . . ." That was right. He had built more than two hundred houses. He had built my parents' white house, just around the curve of the road from his own. He had built his own house again after it was burned. He had even built the parish house for this church, here in the center of town. I didn't listen any more to the sermon; I didn't want to hear about the fear of hell, or even the hope of heaven. The choir sang "Peace Be Still." I sat imagining that I had just run away from home: miles from where I was known I had stolen bread to eat and had been sentenced to five years' hard labor; bare-chested and slick with muscle, I swung the big sledgehammer over my head.

We followed the coffin out and got into a big black car. Crawling through the town and the whole seven miles to the cemetery, we sweated and itched inside the black car. The graveyard was on a hill, and there was a bit of breeze. Two Negroes at the graveside jumped up suddenly when the cars peered over the ridge. They grabbed guiltily at the ground and stuffed things into their pockets; they had been gambling. A mound of red clay sat by the graveside, two shovels protruding from it like antennae from a beetle.

Finally we all stood by the left side of the grave. Mr. Seabury talked softly; it sounded in the heat like the buzzing of a fly in a huge room. They lowered the coffin, the two canvas straps throbbing as they rubbed the baked edges of the grave. ". . . dust . . ." The handful of dropped crumbly red clay spread a shape like a splash of water or a spider on the coffin; the minister's hand was stained by the clay, and it looked as if blood had coiled in his hand and could not be completely washed away.

I pushed two white glass buttons to the center of the marble-top chess table. "I'll raise you two," I said.

He leaned back and threw his cards face up on the table. "No," he said. "I aint got no hand to play with. I've got the same hand I had last time." He turned about and looked over the fields glowing with summer. The thick veins on his bald temples twitched.

I spread his cards out. "Are these really the same cards you had last time?"

"They aint the same cards," he said. "But it's the same hand, all right."

"I don't see how it can be the same hand if it's not the same cards."

"Well, that's something you don't know, then." He picked up his leather fly swatter and slapped at a fly on his knee. "Run fetch me my bottle here," he said, "and bring a clean glass with you."

"Yes sir," I said.

The fire in the little cast-iron stove snuffled and shifted. I climbed on the back of a small straight chair and struck the light bulb which hung suspended on a gilt chain. The shadows in the room lurched alive and began to nod drunkenly. I could count all the gray hairs in my grandmother's head. She sat in a small rocking chair, and I stood behind, towering, it seemed, over her like a giant or as if I were on stilts. I decided that when I grew up I would be very tall; I would be so tall that everyone would just look up at me and do

136

whatever I told them to. I would be red; red-haired and blue-eyed.

"Please don't be hitting that bulb when I'm reading," my grandmother said. She licked a knot on the ball of her thumb and turned a thin page of the Bible. "It makes it hard to see the words with that light going back and forth."

"Yes, mam," I said.

I got down from the chair and went across the room and sat by the drumming stove. A rat-shaped shadow darted in and out under the table: this was the hanging edge of the checked oilcloth. The square-edged shadow of a picture hung on the wall dipped and receded like the sail of a pirate ship. The straight shadow of a chair seat swayed as regularly as a pendulum. My grandmother rocked slightly in her rocking chair, so that its shadow had two motions formed into one, leaning dangerously back and hesitating—as if gathering itself—and then suddenly springing invisible into the chair itself. The clock struck ten.

My grandfather had gone into the icy kitchen for water, and now I heard him coming back. *Bup, swiss, thum.* He came into the room, cold air pouring in behind him through the open door. He closed the door and came across the room. He looked impossibly huge, larger even than my father. I watched him. "You old hoppin Jesus," I said. "You old hoppin Jesus." I said the words idly, without any trace of passion except, perhaps, curiosity. The words were not mine. I had got them from a man I didn't know who had come late one night to this house to use the telephone. He had rank, crisp red hair and flat blue eyes. My grandfather wouldn't let him use the telephone. "You can walk for a telephone," he had said. "It aint but two miles. That aint far for a young feller." Then the red-haired man had said something, and my grandfather had called him a ragged-ass son of a bitch. Then his face had got very red. "You old hopping Jesus," he had said. "You silly old hypocrite." He had shut the door then, disappearing forever. It was as if I had been dreaming him and had suddenly been awakened.

"You old hoppin Jesus," I said. "You old hoppin Jesus."

He stopped, stood dead still. My grandmother looked up from her reading, her mouth slightly open. Everything was silent, except for the drumming of the fire in the stove and the wind outside. "Get up from there," my grandfather said.

"Yes sir," I said. I didn't move.

"You come here. Right now. Right now."

I got up and went to him. I stared at the way his belly bulged over his belt.

"Turn around," he said.

I turned.

Pack. Pack . . . Pack. Two smart burning blows with his cane on my buttocks, one across my back. I broke into silent boiling tears; I didn't turn around.

"You get on into the bedroom now," he said. "You get to bed. I don't want to see no more of you tonight. I don't know how you get such a notion. Right now. Get on."

I pushed blindly into the black hallway that led to the north bedroom, closing the door gently. I rubbed my tears with both hands, wetting my cheeks. It was very cold here away from the stove. I walked down the hallway and went into the bedroom and sat on the bed without turning the light on. I crossed my legs and put my arms between them and sat hunched over in the cold, rocking back and forth on the bed. I kept thinking, Hopping Jesus, hopping Jesus. At first I could

138

see nothing, but at last I became accustomed to the darkness. Through the east window I could see the bare limbs of the apple trees jerk in the wind against the stars. I got up and went to the vanity and looked in the dark mirror at the pale patch of my face. I waited until the sight became clearer and I could make out my features. My eyes were shiny, my mouth looked black. I stared at myself, forcing my mind against the features of my face just as I later forced it against the pine grain in the wall of my bedroom. I willed at my face, to change it. I wanted red hair to sprout, blue walls to click over my any-colored eyes. My eyes were too easily seen through; flat blue eyes were impenetrable. A random scrap of my father's voice floated about in my head: "Your own mother wouldn't recognize you." (*Yes she would, yes she would.*) I looked at the tinted photograph of Roosevelt on the vanity: the features were hard to make out, the face looked as if it were seeping through cloth. I looked out the south window. Uncle had already gone to bed; no lights showed in the tenant house. I turned round and round in the middle of the room, and the windows went by me like windows on a passing train. I began to dance, at first very slowly, but then faster and faster. I lifted my feet and put them down silently. I crouched and leaped up, time and time again. I leaped up as high as I could. I wrapped my arms across my chest and spun round and round up and down the room like a coin set spinning on a table. Then I began to sing silently and the imaginary sound of it was deafening. The silent singing turned into a silent scream which I could feel vibrating in the top of my head. Finally I began to hum aloud, but very quietly. I danced faster and faster until I began to sweat. Then I lay down on the bed. The room turned crazily about me, the windows winking as they passed. I closed my eyes. When at last I opened them, everything had stopped turning. I lay quiet for a moment, then put my hands into my pockets, trying to determine by touch what I was carrying. In one pocket I could feel a perfectly round stone, an empty thread spool, a folded card that I had traded marbles for at school. The friend who had traded with me had been sent it by his father, who was overseas in the Army. In the other pocket I felt three pennies and five fatheaded wooden kitchen matches. I had forgotten that I had the matches; I had stolen them that afternoon while my grandfather was in the living room poking up the fire. The matches were kept in a cabinet in the kitchen. I sat up in the bed, shivering violently after my exertion in dancing. I got up and went over to the vanity again. I struck a match on the floor and held it above my head. My face in the mirror looked yellow and terrifying in the light of the match. I leaned forward and rested my forehead against the chill glass. My image came forward to meet me, like a great fist. I breathed, and my mirrored face fogged to a glowing plane. It was frightening, but I wasn't frightened. Instead, I was joyful, filled with an egoistic glee that I had never felt before. I didn't know what was happening, but I felt exhilarated, fiery. I went to the east window and struck another match. I touched the little flame to both the vague glass curtains that hung on each side of the window, and fire immediately ran upward, blooming yellow and heatless. This illuminated one side of the room. Then I went to the bed and put a lighted match in three places to the fringe of the chenille spread. At first it wasn't going to burn, but then it caught and hands of fire opened upward at the bedside. The room was fantastically lighted now, but I was still cold. I began to try to dance, lifting my feet, cavorting, turning. All the motions. But now the fever had gone out of it. I felt mechanical, passionless. I was still shivering in the cold. Two matches were left. I went to the vanity again. The fire behind me lifted higher, and now I laid on the mirror only a dark, thin image. I set fire to the linen doily on which my grandmother's cosmetics sat and my mirror image sprang back to life. Was it myself there? It seemed I wore a mask which was more angular than my real face and my eyes were blue and I had red hair. But the sight went away, like a mask dissolving instantly, like breath fading from a glass. (*Yes she would.*) "Your own mother wouldn't . . ." (*Yes. Say, Yes.*) I set my last match afire with the flame of the doily and tossed it on top of the chest of drawers. It went out. I wandered to the center of the room and watched the fire spread. The ceiling was quickly blackening with smoke.

I walked down the dark hallway, going back to the living room. I opened and closed the door quickly so that they wouldn't see the flames.

They were exactly as I had left them, except that now my grandfather was sitting down. "You're up kind of early, aint you?" he asked.

"Yes sir," I said.

"Boy, I aint goin to fool with you," he said. "You better get on to bed right now." He surveyed me as I stood shaking by the stove. "Why, you aint even got your nightshirt on yet," he said.

"I was getting ready to go to bed," I said. "I was sitting on the bed and I saw that redheaded man, he came to use the telephone, it was a long time ago, and I waited and just sat there waiting."

"How do you know it was him?" asked my grandfather. "It's pitch dark outside."

141

I couldn't think. "I could just tell," I said. I waited. "What was that last chunk of wood you put in the stove?" my grandfather asked. "Someway, it don't smell right."

"It was just green red oak," I said, waiting. I was glad for the respite, but I was anxious to get it over with. "I just sat there," I said, "and pretty soon the house was on fire. I bet it was him, I'm sure it was."

"The house, you say?"

I went to the hallway door. "This door's already hot," I said. The knob was slippery in my hands.

"Don't you open that door." He stood up painfully as quickly as he could. "I wrote the fire department number on the wall over the phone," he said. "You call that number and tell them to come out here. Then you get everybody's coats out of the closet." My grandmother was standing up now, and he spoke to her. "Mamaw," he said, "hand me down them papers on the mantel."

I didn't stop at the telephone. I ran out the door. Outside, a powdery snow lay on the ground. It was freezing cold. The trees looked pink, and now the points of flame could be seen above the roof. The last star in the Big Dipper was hidden behind Chambers Mountain. I hid behind a walnut tree and poked my head around the rough trunk to see. Light suddenly filled the windows of the house where uncle lived. After a long time my grandparents came through the door of the house, walking very slowly. My grandmother was carrying over her arm my heavy overcoat. I pulled my head in, now completely hidden from them. They walked almost to my tree and stopped. When I peeked out, they had turned around and were watching the fire advance on the healthy part of the house. They stood bent and still, ancient in the fervid light.

142

I heard my grandfather speak. "I guess he's just no-count," he said. "He must be just pure no-count."

Uncle and I had painted the barn twice. Because of the cyclical nature of farm work, we had done almost all our work at least twice. We had painted the roof about a year before my grandfather died, and we painted it again four or five years later when Uncle got out of the Army. About the Army: he wasn't drafted until pretty near the end of the European campaign, and it was his luck to have been drafted, and to receive his basic training just in time for D-day. He pushed across France with the rest of them. His legs were full of shrapnel because he had dived head first into a fox-hole to avoid mortar fire, and his protruding legs had been sprayed with metal fragments. When he came back his legs were dotted with blue lumps, and now and then a shard of shrapnel would work up to the surface of his skin and he would go to a town not far away to the V.A. hospital and have the splinters chopped out. He almost never talked about the war, and it seemed to me then that it had made no impression at all upon him. He had traveled halfway across the world, marching countries I had dreamed of going to since I could remember wishing, but his greatest concerns were still his family, my family, the farm, and his hounds. I could understand it only by telling myself that he wasn't very intelligent, which didn't satisfy me because I knew I was lying to myself. He had taught me too many things: how to harness and manage horses, whether plowing, raking, mowing, discing, or harrowing; how to train a coon dog; how to read trout water; how to cut tobacco and how to chew it; how to hold up a horse's foot to inspect or repair the shoe; how to go behind a strange mule without getting kicked; how to manage—this was later—a tractor, even to back a hay baler into a shed. He taught me how to rob a hive of bees. "Don't be afraid of em at all if you can help it," he said. "If you're a little afraid of em, you won't get bit but once or twice. Whatever you do, honey, don't go out to rob your bees on election day. They won't bite a man that's scared too much, but a man that's mad, they'll cover him up in a minute."

Once we were in the woods, training a new hound pup. In the middle of the trail we found a mud puddle. He stopped. "Wait a minute," he said. "Hold on to that dog. I hadn't never thought what a good place this was." We squatted on our heels. He kept watching the puddle. In a few minutes, a bee dropped to the ground and crawled to the puddle edge to drink. "Keep your eye on him," he said. "Help me keep him sighted." Shortly, the bee flitted away. "Let's go," Uncle shouted.

We ran down the side of the mountain at breakneck speed. I had never run so fast in my life. We thrashed through laurel bushes, jumped over decaying logs, scrambled on our hands and knees down rock piles. I fell twice, rolling over and over in damp oak leaves and ferns and pine needles, and got up in time to glimpse Uncle's disappearing heels in the underbrush. At last I caught up with Uncle, who had stopped on the edge of a stand of tall oaks. We had run about a quarter of a mile. I was winded, gasping. He held up his hand. We listened: a steady drone as of a far-distant airplane. He pointed out a tree in the middle of the small grove. We could see bees circling about a limb near the top of the tree.

"We'll have us some new bees and some new honey too. This wild kind's sweeter than hive honey," he said.

144

I was truly astonished. "I don't see how you could follow that bee," I said. "I don't see how you could keep your eye on it."

"They aint no need to see it," he said. "You don't need to see nothin but the way it heads, because a bee always travels in a straight line from the watering place."

"How come you were running so fast, then? I thought you were trying to keep up with the bee."

"You got to travel fast because you want to go in a straight line," he said. "If you go slow, you'll try to find the easy way around a thicket or a rock pile. Then you'll be off of your bee line. If you want to go straight to it, you got to go as fast as you can, and not go around or double back or nothin."

We sat on a log and took out cigarettes. By now I had learned to smoke pretty well.

"Now, don't translate this literally," my father said. "I mean, don't try to, because I know you can't translate literally in the first place because you don't know enough Latin, and I suspect in the second place you don't know enough English to understand your own translation, even if it is literal." He glanced idly at the book held open on his knees. "O.k. Listen:

> Auream quisquis mediocritatem
> Diligit, tutus caret obsoleti
> Sordibus tacti, caret invidenda
> Sobrius aula.

Just tell me in your own words, or anyway words you think are your own, what you think he's talking about."

"Well," I said, "he says uh that the man that uh sticks to the golden mean and uh isn't too poor or too

145

rich uh isn't hurt by the uh trouble uh the poor man or the rich man has."

"Auream mediocritatem," he said. "What does that mean?"

"The golden mean."

"What does that mean, the golden mean?"

"It means, I guess sort of about the middle," I said. "Not too rich, not too poor."

"Do you mean *bourgeois?*" he asked. "Or *petty bourgeois* maybe?"

"Yes sir," I said hopefully.

He closed the book. "You don't know much, do you?" he asked.

"No sir," I said.

A January. It was very cold. It was horrible. My sister wouldn't come with me back to the house out of the cold. "Come on," I told her. "Come on, Julia." She was still whimpering. Her hands were scarlet, small, fat. I touched her hand with my fingers and it felt like paper. It felt as if it might crinkle and tear. There were small tears in her eyes, and her face was scared. The moonlight made very tiny triangular patches on her tears.

I started back. The road was full of frozen rocks. Once I didn't hear her whimpering and I looked and she was sitting in the road. I took her elbows and lifted her up. She was terribly heavy, and she didn't want to stand. She wouldn't stiffen her knees. I held her up that way for a long time. "Come on, Julia," I said. "You'll freeze to death if you don't come on."

We went a short way, but when she saw the log by the road that was used for a chopping block she went to it and sat down. She wasn't whimpering now, but

146

her eyes had become larger. They seemed as large as eggs; they seemed not to belong to her face. "Please come on," I said. "You'll freeze to death out here. Please."

She kept staring at me. I pulled at her. Her wrists felt glassy under my fingers, like ice without moisture on it. "What are you doing?" I asked, crying. "Please. Why won't you come on? You'll freeze to death. Please." I couldn't make her move. I was terrified because I thought she had frozen to the log.

It got later and later. The moon was larger and yellower.

I pulled at her again and again. She wouldn't move. Her face still turned up to me. The two tears were still there. She looked transmuted, statuelike, in the yellow moonlight. I kept thinking, Something awful, something.

"Why don't you leave her alone? What makes you hurt her?"

My father suddenly appeared behind me. In the moonlight he looked like a giant. He too had a small tear in each eye. The front of his big mackinaw went out and in as he breathed heavily. His breath came white in the air and then floated away upward.

"What are you doing to her? What gets into you?"

She raised her arms, and he stooped to her, and she crawled against him like a small animal crawling into a nest. She drew herself into a bundle, her arms brought to her chest, her knees drawn against her arms. He carried her carefully. He seemed reverent.

He turned his back to me and walked away, taking long steps worth four of mine. Sometimes I had to run to catch up, and I kept alternating my gait all the way home.

"Open the door," my father said hoarsely. He rapped

147

the door with the toe of his heavy shoe.

My mother opened the door. She looked through my head at my sister, red in my father's arms. "What were they doing?" she asked. Her mouth thinned, her jaw hardened. "What happened?"

I went to the brown enameled coal stove and put my hand flat against its side. It was a long time before I felt the heat. My face began to itch, and I rubbed it with both hands. Then I walked to the east window and looked at the moon, huge and yellow, snared in the skinny maple branches.

Julia began to cry. She cried louder and louder. She cried until she gagged for breath. "They hurt him," she cried. "They made him pull his drawers down. They made him do bad." Now she was almost screaming. "They wouldn't let him."

My father's footsteps made the room rattle. A dim spot emerged from the pane as I breathed, and I stood there and it got larger and larger, like a gray flower unfolding. My father's huge presence made the back of my neck prickle. His hand closed hard on my shoulder. It was as if my shoulder had been pinned by a heavy door.

"What happened? What's the matter?"

My breath had obscured the whole window pane, clouding away the world of the night outside.

In those days I spent a great deal of time thinking about my death. I suppose this is a rather typical concern of the pale adolescent who is left too often to his own devices. (*Do you have horrible thoughts?* the personality tests ask, and the future drunkard or the future college professor answers, *Well, what other kinds are there?*) It seems strange to me now that I should have thought about my death in those days only because—I believe—I never do any more. On the other hand, I think about things now that I never thought about then. Time, for instance. I watch fascinated as the weeks and months reel away like a line that a big fish has snapped up, and now it seems frightening, incomprehensible. But then I knew time only by seasons: snow season, fence-building season, hay season, school season. The only way I could measure time then was by the weight of my epic poem. It finally ran to fourteen hundred handwritten pages, to Galaxy Six, Constellation Three, Sector Six. I began it about the middle of my ninth year, and I don't know when I stopped writing at it. When I went away to college it was lost, and although I searched strenuously for it during the Easter vacation of my freshman year, I could find no trace. I suspect that my father burned it.

I remember that my grandfather used to shave with a straight razor. He would prop a small, slightly concave mirror on the chess table he had made, and hold in his lap a bowl of hot water. For soap he used only regular bar soap, so that there was never a lather on his face, but only a film of soap, like the film of wetness on an iced drink glass. He scraped and scratched until he had satisfied himself, and then he called me to take his tools away. I would pour the greasy, specked water into the toilet, and then rinse the bowl out at the lavatory. Then I would dry it with a towel and put the folded razor into it and take mirror, razor, and bowl to the closet in the little blue living room and set them on the top shelf.

The single time I decided to commit suicide—I don't know how old I was then, but I'm pretty sure I wasn't yet thirteen—I chose the straight razor as tool. I took both the razor and the blue earthenware bowl upstairs

149

to the south bedroom. Somehow I had heard—my father must have told me—of the death of Petronius. I would drain myself away sweetly and calmly and wittily. They would find me white and dry with a book open in my lap. I spent a long time deciding which book to die with. I finally decided upon a large purple-bound copy of Victor Hugo, the Selected Works. I had never read Hugo, but I knew he was supposed to be great literature, and that served my purpose. They would find me with my blood in the shaving bowl, and my lap full of purple Hugo. Among my effects ("effects," that was the word) they would find the first two hundred seventeen pages of my great unfinished poem. Then they would be sorry.

It was already late in the afternoon. I set the bowl on the vanity in the south bedroom. I opened the razor and laid it beside the bowl. The thin, stropped edge of the blade looked painful and horrifying. I looked at myself in the mirror for a long time. I was very sad. Finally I opened the volume of Hugo. It was the middle of *The Hunchback*, and I turned back to the beginning. I would read a few sentences, get rid of some blood, read some more, let more blood, until at last there wouldn't be any more blood. I began.

Two hours later I had to stop reading. The light of the sunset had failed completely; the room was getting cold. I took one of the match covers I had collected that day and put it into the book to keep my place. I folded the razor and put it back into the bowl and carried everything down into the living room.

My grandfather laughed when he saw me. "You aint got any need for that," he said. "They aint a hair on you but what's on your head. You're awful little to start shavin."

I just then remembered that I had set out to kill myself. Suddenly I was furious. I lifted the bowl above my head and smashed it to the floor. Splinters flew, the folded razor spun across the room. "That's what," I cried elliptically.

"I don't know what gets into you," he said. "That aint no way to act."

14

TUESDAY MORNING. While I'm packing my suitcase the telephone rings. Sylvia comes into the bedroom to tell me that it's for me.

"Hello."

"James? This is Arvin." Reynolds, the editor for Winton Press.

"How are you?"

"I'm calling because I have this letter here from you."

"Yes."

"Asking for an application blank. Hell, James, you know you don't need to apply again. Just come on back to your office."

"I thought I'd better fill out the blank and everything."

"No reason to," he says. "Just show up for work. We hadn't even thought of hiring anybody else as long as you were free. You'll be paid for your work on the tobacco disease book too. Don't worry about it, just come on back."

"Well, if you don't mind, I mean, if it's not too much trouble, I'd rather fill out the blank and everything."

"Why?"

"I don't know. I'd really rather have it that way, though."

"Well, if that's what you want," he says. I can almost

hear him scratching his head.

"If I had my druthers," I say.

"O.k., then. I'll just bring it by your place on my way from work. No use wasting a day with the mails."

"Don't bother with that. Just drop it in the mail. I'm going to be gone a few days anyway, so I wouldn't be here. It would have to wait anyway."

"Well. All right then. I'm glad you're coming back with us, James. We have some new things coming up. The stuff looks better now than it has in a long while."

"That's good news," I say. "I'll send in the blank just as soon as I get back."

"Fine," he says. "You be careful now."

"Yes. We'll see you."

Going back to the bedroom, I stop by my study. Perhaps I ought to carry something to read with me. The study is clean and bare, surgical. Only the desk, the chair, the typewriter, a square of typewriter paper and a layer of manuscript, and seven or eight novels by H. G. Wells on one of the shelves. I ponder, and finally choose *When the Sleeper Wakes*. Optimistic title.

At last I snap the suitcase shut. Sylvia sits in the chair at the vanity, watching me. "Is that all you need?" she asks dubiously.

"Yes," I say. "I'm not going to be gone that long."

She rasps at a fingernail with a sandy file. "I'm so glad you're going," she says. "Your folks will be so glad to see you."

"I guess so."

"There's a box Julia wants you to take. I put it in the living room."

"How did she know I was going up home?"

"Oh, I called her last night," Sylvia says. "She brought the box right over. It's just a few things she wants your mother to keep for her. She was going to

153

mail it, but since you're going. It's just a small box, it won't be in your way."

"No, that's all right." Momentarily vexed. "Well . . ." I heft the bag up. "I'd better get started."

She rises. "The box is in the living room. I'll bring it out. Don't you want to say goodbye to John and Missy?"

"No," I say. "No use getting them all upset. I'll sneak off and they won't know I'm gone."

The package is small. Sylvia puts it in the back seat of the Ford. I toss my suitcase into the trunk. "Well, goodbye," I say. "You be careful, now."

"*You* be careful." A firm kiss on my lips. A taste faintly reminiscent of raspberries. Again, "*You* be careful."

"I will."

In the rear-view mirror I see her waving and I put my hand out the window and wave back. It's a bright morning, but not very hot yet. The brightness won't bother me for a while yet because the sun will be behind me or overhead until mid-afternoon. I head northwest out of town at a moderate rate of speed. I can't go too fast because I'm not familiar with the roads. The highways have changed quite a bit since I used to drive home for the holidays from Winton College. It's only about three hundred miles, from the middle of the state to the western end, but it's been six years since I've been home. A new four-lane highway now running over half the distance. In fact, I haven't seen my parents in five years. The last time I saw them was that day Sylvia and I were married in Winton North Central Methodist Church. My father had already stopped teaching, and was taking care of the farm. "I'm retired now," he had said. "I'm just farming." It was the first time he had met Sylvia, whom I had dated in

154

college. He was gracious enough, but seemed basically uninterested. He gave me a calloused handshake after the wedding: the farmwork had put horn on his palms. "Take care of yourself now," he had said. Goodbyes all around. It was the last time I had seen him; he seemed curiously aloof to me, to everyone, since my grandmother had died during my junior year at college. We hadn't written or called each other these five years now, and I was going home to see him and my mother before I started work again.

The landscape looks bright and fresh scooting by, and the road isn't too crowded. I drive steadily westward, beginning myself to wish for a radio in the car. The soil and the smell of it begin to change. The white eastern sand gives way to red, shaly clay, a sharper, but not so clean, odor. At Salisbury, a baked, minuscule town, blue clumps of mountains appear, thrusting the sunlit distance forward. I stop for a beer and a sandwich at a small brick roadside joint. It's about two o'clock, and I sit for another hour watching soap operas on the small television set canted dangerously over the top of the bar mirror. It's cool enough in here so that I leave reluctantly. But at last I do leave.

No serious trouble until I get to my home town. I find then that I've actually forgotten which road to take out of town to get to the farm. It seems fantastic. Finally I have to stop at a grocery store to ask directions. And get them only after having been well punctured with suspicious glances. So that it's almost dark by the time I do get to the big brick house, the mountains to the west shutting away the last minutes of sunset. I park the Ford behind the house and, seeing no lights, get out. Sweat glues the back of my shirt and pants and underwear to my skin, and at first I walk with a numb unsteadiness after the long drive. I'm very tired, but the cool, faintly moist air is good. I walk around toward the front of the house, leaving my suitcase and Julia's box until later.

I see a cigarette glowing on the front porch in the dimness, and hear a low cough, almost like a chuckle. The broad seated form of—I suppose—my father. I go up the cement steps. "Hello," I say.

"Hello," says my father. "How was the trip?"

"O.k., I guess. How did you know I was coming?"

"Your wife called this morning. We've been watching for you. Did you have your supper yet? Your mother has some for you in the refrigerator." His voice sounds the same as it always has, but perhaps a bit lazier and more preoccupied. A good voice for reading Tennyson.

"Well, that sounds good," I say. "Is Mother here?"

"She'll be here after a while. She's gone to her church circle meeting. Or maybe she's gone to class tonight. I always manage to forget which night is which on her schedule, although I suppose it doesn't really make any difference. We're pretty well past the age of expecting emergencies now, so I'm sure I don't need to get in touch with her in any great hurry. Unless, of course, there is an emergency right now, your coming here." This was a question. "Why don't you sit down?" he asks.

I sit gingerly opposite him in a squeaking metal lawn chair. "No," I say, "no emergency. I just thought I'd come up for a visit."

"That's fine," he says. "You're on vacation then, I take it."

"Sort of."

The cigarette reddens in a last puff and then arcs off the porch into the darkness. "That's what I thought.

Julia wrote us a couple of times about your not working, and for no good reason as far as she could see. As far as I can see, either. I take it you didn't come up to see me about getting a job. I don't remember your ever showing much talent for anything besides sedentary labor. A few days working in the fields will come nearer killing you than putting you in condition for more."

"You don't want me to come up here, then."

"Oh yes," he says. "I'm looking forward to that day when you do come. That is, whenever I think you've come, and haven't escaped or been driven up here. I mean, when you come like somebody who has come to visit, with your wife and your family with you. In fact, we've had some little trouble waiting for you. It's not that much fun for us, waiting for four or five or however many years to see our grandchildren. I don't suppose we are going to wait much longer. In fact, your mother and I have been thinking of having your wife up here a few weeks. Maybe a few months or a year or two would be better. In the first place, I don't like to think about your kids inheriting your hatred—or do they call it an allergy now?—whatever—of clean air and sunlight. But if they do come, I want *them*. And every time I see you around I'll just try to drive you off with a shotgun."

"Why?"

"Well, that's hyperbole, of course. I don't like the thought of turning a gun on a mewling baby, especially one over thirty years old. What I can't understand is how you ever thought of coming up here. You could have everything that's on my mind, and I believe I can speak pretty fairly for your mother too, over the telephone in a few minutes."

"I don't know."

"The only thing I could figure was that you've been reading too many novels. Telemachus. Stephen Dedalus. The boy with the golden screw for a navel. The search for a father. All that literary stuff. I've read it myself, one time or another. It's hogwash. Bull shit. I've just about stopped reading, and only just now I've started hoping that I've stopped in time. Even our damn barn cat has got enough sense to chase its younguns off when they get old enough. The next time that bunch of cats meet, they can meet on respectable terms. They're smart, smarter than most of us. At least they know what a family is for. Because the family isn't something you give your life to. Not unless you want to see your children turn out bloodsuckers, sucking the juice out of you. It's something you put your life into, like an incubator maybe, and you can hope that it will hatch out stronger than it was before. I suppose that makes no sense at all, because I know me. I'll generally clutter up what I want to say with words. I talk too damn fancy. But that's all right because I know you too. If what I was saying was a piece of iron I could hit you with, I couldn't get you to understand me still. Not even if I could brand it on your hide."

"You want me to go back, then? I'll leave right now."

A long pause; perhaps he's reflecting. "You'll do better to leave about noon tomorrow," he says. "Your supper's in the refrigerator. You can sleep upstairs."

I go in and take out of the refrigerator a cold plate covered over with waxed paper. Fresh buttermilk out of a jar. A predictable meal: fried chicken, green beans, sliced tomatoes, sliced cucumbers. Cornbread on top of the electric stove. During the meal a faint, but familiar, odor worries me, and it's not until I go through the living room into the dark hallway that leads to the

158

stairs that I recognize it. An odor like the odor of wet ashes, the smell of a burned house.

I go up the stairs to my old bedroom and turn on the light. Not much change: the two great beds at right angles to each other, the black desk between them. Pine slatting walls painted white. Empty bookshelves against the north walls: these used to hold the books and magazines that Sylvia threw away only the other day. The room is clean, but a bit musty. I go to the gabled windows and open both of them. The cool night streams on my face and body. I need a bath, but it's too much trouble. Plumbing has rarely worked in this house anyway. Coming back from the windows, I snag myself on the finishing nail sticking in the corner of the desk. My grandmother's notes to me used to hang here. I never used to snag myself, but of course I was smaller then. The room seems much smaller too, now.

Nothing to read. Too much trouble to go back after my suitcase. I sit on the right-hand bed smoking, and take off my shoe and use it for an ash tray. At last I strip and go to the door and turn the light out and come back to the bed. The sheets are cool, dampish, slightly musty. I'm very tired, but not really sleepy. I lie awake, a sensation on my eyes of everything running past me, the effect of driving all day. A long drive that came to an abrupt, and, yes, a disappointing end. I lie thinking. For a while I try very hard to deceive myself that my father is arrogant in presuming that I had come to see him. But even now I know that he's right. He is right: I ought to square away; straighten up and fly right, Preach says, keep your eyes open. I myself have written once in trying to pull things together in some manner, "Take yourself up." But after all I'm weary of making resolutions that I have no strength, and not even any real desire, to keep. I really don't see how I'm going to get up the moxie to make any more resolutions. Where does it get you? Step up, step down, step up, step down. Think of a neon light blinking on and off. Perhaps, though, after all, I didn't come up merely to see my father; this was only a part of it. I wanted to see the farm and the house again, and to remember in some measure what has happened. I don't think I want to live any longer in the way I do; my present way of living has made this crazy hash out of my past life. Isn't it true that if I could get my past settled in the right groove my present life would trundle along the way it's supposed to? It's like getting a nut cross-threaded on a bolt: you have to twist it back and try until it fits correctly. I don't want to think about it.

Footsteps on the stairs, and a light rap at the door. Hesitantly, a second lighter tap.

"Yes?" I ask.

Sound of the door opening. "Well, so you've come at last." My mother's voice, gay and a bit strained from climbing the stairs. Her form is barely distinguishable in the dark, a dark shape in the darker shape of the door. Symbolic as hell, I think, irritated now.

"I guess so."

"How are you?"

"Fine."

"How are Sylvia and the children?"

"Fine."

Her slight chuckle. "It's not much fun just to talk in the dark. I'll let you sleep in a moment. I can see you in the morning, when you're rested."

"That's all right," I say. "I'm not sleepy."

It seems she settles herself more comfortably in the doorway. "Well, I didn't want to bother you, but your father sent me up as a sort of messenger boy, I think."

"What does he want?"

"The trouble is, I don't know," she says. "He seems to think he may have disturbed you by something he said when you got here. I think I'm supposed to let you know he's still your good buddy. What were you-all talking about, anyway?"

"Nothing," I say. ". . . Cats, I guess."

Her light, clear giggle sounds fresh in the dark, a swallow of cool water. "Is he still talking about those cats? He's been griping a month about that silly barn cat. He won't let it come near him; he says it's an unnatural animal that won't take care of its young. 'It's a goddamn *lusus naturae.*' If he's said that once, he's said it a hundred times. Couldn't you-all find anything better to talk about, after all this time?"

"I don't know," I say. "It's hard to talk to him."

"Oh, it's not hard. Your father's got it in his head that the only way a real masculine man ought to talk is in grunts and profanity. But the trouble is, he likes to talk too much for that to satisfy him. So he runs on. I've lived with him long enough to know he doesn't mean anything he says for an hour at a time. When he says 'logic,' he means love, and when he says 'good sense,' he means love. It's just the word that scares him. Every now and then, I like to say 'love' to him just to watch him jump. He almost jumps out of his skin." She laughs lightly. "I bet if I said 'love' three times in a row, he'd faint dead away."

"Maybe so."

"I'll let you sleep now," she says. A last word edges through the closing door: "Cats . . ." The door muffles a giggle.

I lie there. Once I almost fell asleep, but I have one of those awful sensations of running and running that

161

one often has before falling asleep. A fence looms up that I have to jump, and I jerk in the bed, startling myself wide-eyed in a cold sweat. The roosters have already begun crowing, but I still lie there waiting. I crane my neck and see that the stars have moved. At last I get up and strike a match to look at my watch. I light a cigarette and slip down the stairs and out of the house. I take Julia's box out of the back seat and put it on the porch. Then I go back to the car and drive away. It is about three-thirty.

An hour and a half later I realized that I've taken a wrong turn at some point. The sun is up now and everything is fresh in the new day. Smell of mown grass in the wind through the car window. But this isn't the road that I came up on. I'm headed east, though, the right direction, so I decide to keep on until I can get information. Finally I come to a little town called Pinecrest, and get a map at a service station. I find that I'm only about twenty miles south of the four-lane highway that leads to Winton. Across the street from the gas station is a brick hotel. Ambassador Hotel. It has a restaurant on the ground floor, and I cross the street for breakfast after parking my car in the gas station parking lot. It's pretty bad: heavy pancakes, limp bacon, bitter coffee. Then I go to the desk in the hotel lobby and take a single room, no bath. Three dollars.

The room is gray all over, including the bed linen. But there are large rust-colored spots on the wallpaper. The room is bare as a picked skeleton: wall mirror, desk, night stand, bed. Two lamps, three ash trays, one Gideon Bible. I pile on the bed still fully clothed and go to sleep.

I wake up at four o'clock in the afternoon. This is lunchtime, but the hotel dining room is closed. Opens at five, the desk clerk tells me. I buy new cigarettes and

162

go back to my room. I look out the window. Pinecrest crawls sluggishly about in the mounting June heat. I smoke and watch the windows of advancing cars blaze and die as they move in and out of the correct angle to the sun. My mouth feels as if it were crusted; too many cigarettes. I call and send the bellhop out for bourbon and ice, and tip him a dollar.

By five o'clock I'm nearly drunk and, although I don't particularly want to eat, go down to the dining room anyway. I eat something, I don't know or care what, and go back to the room. I sit awhile with the bourbon, watching the words of Acts creep bloated up the page. Then I go to bed, snatching an hour here and there between chapters of the Bible, until four A.M., when I drop off for good. I wake at two o'clock the next day feeling pretty good, and leave just as I am.

—So that when I get to Winton, about six o'clock, my headache throbs and burns and my mouth feels sore from smoking. I decide to have a beer before going home, and I park in front of Troy's Grill. Sitting in one of the booths is Mavis and a man whom I've never met. I smile and nod to her, hoping to pass with this, but she stops me. "Well, you son of a bee-itch," she says. "I hope you're sorry now."

"Hello, Mavis. Sorry for what?"

"For what you done," she says, snapping chewing gum.

"What did I do?"

"To Preacher." Her escort has glanced at me once, and now takes care not to look in my direction. He probably has me figured for a rival. Mavis is wearing a fuzzy pink sweater, her small breasts letting fall a shadow like beard stubble.

"What happened to Preacher?"

"You know just like everybody else what happened

163

to Preacher. You were at the party last night, weren't you? Judy said you and her left together right before Jack Davis come in. She's right too, because if you-all hadn't of left, it would be you lyin there in the hospital, it wouldn't be Preacher."

"Why? I wasn't at a party last night. I wasn't even in town."

"Judy said you and her went to a party." She nods musingly. "You-all had better get together on your stories before you go around talkin."

"It's not true, though."

"I don't know," she says, "but I guess it's the truth that she'll tell you just about anything. I guess I know that's so. Anyway, Preacher is in the hospital because Jack Davis come to that party and busted his head till he's just about dead."

"That's Judy's husband, Jack Davis?"

"Don't you know him? I thought you'd know him. I thought just about everybody would know him." She nods again. "That's who it is, all right. That son of a bee-itch."

"No, I don't know him."

"Well, he's in the jailhouse now," she says. "Chuck's wife called the cops as soon as he come in and started botherin Preacher. But they was too late, they couldn't nobody stop him once he come after him. Preacher knew it, too." All this rings of direct quotation from Judy.

"Oh." I find that I don't want beer after all. As I leave the place I get a newspaper out of the vending rack. Then I drive home.

Sylvia finishes up with the kids, feeds them, bathes them, puts them to bed. Then she comes back to fix my meal.

164

"I just want sandwiches," I say.

"There's salami and cheese and some tuna salad," she says.

"Fine." I sit at the table in the kitchenette, drinking coffee and looking at my newspaper.

"How was the trip?" she asks.

"O.k."

"How are your folks?"

"Just fine."

"I'll bet they were glad to see you."

"Oh yes. Look," I say, jabbing the paper with my finger, "I can't understand these headlines. 'Lawyer, Judge Part on School Prayer.' What does that mean? 'Soblen Tries to Kill Self, Not Jail.' What's that about?"

She places two sandwiches before me. "It's just news-paperese," she says. "Headlinese. You have to keep reading the paper constantly to understand the headlines. If you don't, it's like coming in in the middle of a story. You have to keep up."

"Do you understand this?" I point at "Thirst-Ridden Prisoner Off Water Tower."

"That must be about those three men in the prison riot," she says.

"You must keep up pretty well, then."

"I usually watch the morning news on TV."

After I eat the sandwiches, I suddenly feel too tired to sit up. On my way to the bedroom, I open the door to the study. As clean and bare as a pool table. Sylvia is at my elbow. "You didn't really want me to throw your things out, did you?"

"Oh yes." Then, "No, I guess not, really." The admission makes me feel guilty.

"I knew you didn't."

"That's all right," I say. "Right now I just want to go to bed."

"I'll turn it down for you."

165

Just before I fall asleep, I hear her walking about in the attic, dragging at some sort of box or trunk. Then no more.

The next morning I fill out the job application blank that the Press has sent and drop it into a corner mailbox on my way to the hospital where Preacher must be. One hospital in seventy miles. Bright day, not too hot yet. As I pass the Winton campus I see girls strolling about in sun dresses, books in their arms. I had forgotten that summer school has started.

Judy is in the room with Preach. She wears a white, lumpy blouse, and the kind of short skirt heavy girls shouldn't wear. Her crossed ham bulges on her knee like spilling Jello. Preach lies in the sheets asleep or unconscious, pale and icy-looking. His red hair isn't visible. A bandage covers all his head above his eyebrows.

"Is he going to be all right?" I ask her.

Judy tosses her *True Confessions* on the window sill. "A goddamn lot you care about it," she says. "If it wasn't for you he wouldn't be here. If he was to die you're the one I'll hold to blame for it."

"Why?" I'm truly puzzled. "He isn't going to die," I say.

She glances at his stiff face. "Well, I just hope not," she says. "It's all your fault in the first place."

"What does the doctor say?"

She holds air in her cheeks so that her puffy face looks bigger and rounder, and then lets it out in what among her gestures passes for a sigh. "They won't tell *me* nothin," she says, "because I aint his sister or nothin. That doctor, he don't like me anyway. Well, I don't like him either and I aint afraid to tell him

166

about it. He don't scare me none, his big ways."

"There really isn't a chance of his dying, is there?"

"I don't know, but I wouldn't be surprised. They say he was beat up somethin awful." She looks at his face again, measuring the life in him. "It wouldn't surprise me none. It'll be on your head if he does."

"Why?"

She looks at me angrily. "Well, it was you that Jack come after. If he'd of knew it, it was you he wanted to be laid out. You're just lucky is all. I told him when he come tellin me what he heard that it was that Preacher started tellin all that stuff just so he could cover up for tryin to get with me hisself. It's the truth, is what I told him, that Preacher spends half his time moonin around here. You can't get rid of him for love or money, I said, I can't hardly even get my housework done, much less these two younguns waited on. I told him straight out about how Preacher kept on tryin to get me to go with him to this party last night and I wouldn't. Which party, was what he asked me. He jumped up like he'd been shot. I told him I thought it was Chuck something or other, I didn't know. All I know was Preacher kept tryin to get me to go with him. Then he said at least he'd know where to find that redheaded son of a bitch. Then he told me when the cops come around to say I hadn't seen him. I told him they'd done been around twice, he better make tracks too, because they'll keep comin back till they do find you, I said."

"Mavis said that you told her you and I went to the party together."

"That Mavis," she says, blinking her eyes, "she'll tell you anything, just the first thing that comes in her head. How would she know anything, I wonder. She wasn't even at the house last night. She was layin out somewhere, with that new feller, I bet. What was his name?

Sonny, I believe. She don't know nothin about it at all."

I notice that Preacher's mouth has begun to move, opening and closing silently, his thin lips pursing slightly, like an eye squinting. Then his face is still again. What if he really is going to die? A ghoulish feeling, to be standing here squabbling with Judy. I suddenly have the feeling that she and the form of Preacher lying there and Mavis are strangers to me. I don't know them. I would never have the chance to know them; my life isn't headed in the right direction ever to know them, or even to meet them. I remember how I have often sat in the summer afternoons on the porch of our house in the suburbs. Directly across the street from our house lives an elderly couple, the man now retired. They still have many friends left them, frequent visitors, who take long goodbyes on their front porch while I sit across the street drinking bourbon and watching. "Say hello to John and his family for me when you see them." "Did you know the Watermans have bought a new house?" "Her second daughter starts in college this fall." "Well, goodbye now, yes, goodbye." I know a good deal about these visitors without even having met them, an observer in the hidden cave of anonymity. Isn't this how I am related to Judy and Preach and Mavis, merely as a tolerably interested observer? I don't really know them; they certainly don't know me. It will simplify things for me just to forget the whole business. When I start back to work, it will all be over. They'll never see me again.

Judy has been talking. ". . . that's what I should have done. But if I'd of told him about you, I don't know what. He don't even know you. I bet he never even heard about you because he's been on the roads a long time now."

"Preacher told me your husband knew all about me," I say. Her puffy face swells and reddens as if it might explode. Her eyes become smaller. I can't tell if it's maddened grief or pure anger. "I don't care," she cries. "I don't care nothin about you. It was Preacher I really like. It was him all the time."

When I get back home from the hospital I spend the rest of the morning playing in the back yard with the children. I toss a rubber ball to John and he throws it heartily, but not accurately, back. I swing Missy on one of the swings of the gym set. Here are the ball and the swing, both going back and forth, back and forth. About twelve-thirty we all sit down to eat together. After lunch Sylvia puts them both away for the afternoon nap. I sit for a second cup of coffee and when she comes back she asks, "Why don't you take a nap now, too? Or go and rest a while in your study."

"Maybe I'll take a nap," I say.

When I look in on the study a few minutes later, I see that all the old stuff has been put back. Here are the books and the old pulp magazines, the railroad flare, the parts of the radio, even the thread spools. It isn't all piled together now, but laid neatly article by article on the shelves and on the desk. It's like a man dissected and laid out bone by bone, nerve by nerve. Already I feel much better, almost happy.

I call to Sylvia, and she comes, drying her soapy hands on an apron. "I thought you threw all this stuff away," I say. "I didn't know you'd kept it."

"I knew you really didn't want to get rid of it," she says. "I just stored it in the attic. I brought it down last night after you went to bed."

"Oh."

She looks up at me gravely. "Are you glad it's still here?"

I put my hand on the back of her neck, stroking her hair. She leans her head against my arm. "Yes," I say.

"We'll be all right, won't we?" she asks.

"Maybe," I say. "I don't know."

"I think so," she says. "Why don't you just rest in here for a while?" She closes the door after her.

I light a cigarette and sit down at the desk. After a while I roll a sheet of paper into the typewriter. I look at it for a time, but the thought of writing anything makes my stomach jerk and fight. Sour foretaste of vomiting. I tear the paper out and throw it on the floor. Then I walk about the room, looking at each object separately. Broken slingshot, chips of records, flashlight batteries. Stamps. Diminished baseball. Code of Conduct card; I read rule number two: *I will never surrender of my own free will.* No. A solemn promise. Never to surrender. Broken fishing reel, bottle of model airplane glue. Curled photographs. At last I pick up *The War of the Worlds* and read in it toward the end until I doze off in the chair at the desk.

Sylvia awakens me after a while, saying, "It's for you." Her head just around the half-opened door.

"What?"

"Telephone," she says.

I follow her into the kitchen and pick up the receiver.

"I told you he was goin to die," Judy says. Her voice is scratchy. "I knew he was goin to, but no, you wouldn't pay me no mind. Well, if you think for one minute that I'm—"

"It's not my fault," I say. "It's not my fault."

Sponge in hand, Sylvia stands up from cleaning the oven. She watches me, standing with her legs spread. Her eyes are fearful.

170

"Well, I'd like to know whose fault it is then. I'd like to know who you think started the whole thing."

"He did," I say. "It wasn't me, it wasn't even any of my business."

"Well, Mr. High and Mighty, you just think you're smart, that's all," says Judy. "Because you've got yours coming, buddyro. You'll get yours, by God."

"Goodbye," I say. "I'm going to hang up."

"Don't you hang up on me," she says. "You just better not."

"Goodbye," I say. I settle the receiver in the cradle and lean against the wall. "Oh Jesus."

Sylvia puts her hand on my arm. "What is it? James?"

"I don't care," I say. I turn from the wall, and stare closely into her face. "It's not your fault when you do something you have to do, what you can't help. There's no sin in it, then."

"What do you mean? I don't know what you're talking about."

"It's nothing," I say. She presses her hand on the back of my head. "Yes, it is, too," I say. I begin talking. In three minutes, I have told her the whole story.

"It's not your fault," she says. "You don't have to feel bad about it, or guilty."

"I don't feel bad," I say. "I feel happy. I feel better, like I had chains taken off me. I feel like I just burned down a house with all the bad things in the world in it."

"That's good," she says. "That's good, James. I'm glad you don't feel sorry."

"I feel sorry," I say, "I feel worse about it than anything."

"You shouldn't. I'm glad you told me," she says. "I'm awfully glad you told me."

Suddenly, like a light snapped on, all my thinking stops. "Yes," I say. "I'm glad too."

171

THREE DREAMS recur frequently:

In a bar, well but softly lighted, a bar not at all like Troy's Grill, but one like those bars in the plush Technicolor movies where the famous novelist's wife goes to arrange adultery. Cool green plants growing about. Uniformed bartenders. I sit on a cushioned stool, drinking something pleasant and nonalcoholic. Preach sits on a stool beside me, turned toward me. He is dressed in a gray, immaculate Brooks Brothers suit. Thin lapels, small cuff links. He talks to me in a low, genially confident voice, speaking correct, and, it seems to me, elegant English. "You must somehow train yourself to become aware of the world you make and which is made for you," he says. "You really must learn to open your eyes to what goes on within you and around you. And you must stop yourself thinking that when I burned down the house of your forefathers it was either the end or the beginning of things. Your life will never be presented to you in those kinds of terms." He leans closer, his voice intimating friendship, respect, and a touch of pity. "You know it too," he says confidently. This assertion does not startle me, but I look into the wide bluish mirror behind the bar, trying to unriddle the expression on his face. As I look, it becomes clear to me that we both are wearing masks and wigs. His mask is jagged in a simulation of his bony face; my mask is glassy in an imitation of my own smooth, characterless face. The white-coated bartender comes from behind the bar to stand at our backs, and then, smoothly and professionally—as if it were a part of his job—he take Preacher's mask off and claps it on my face, and puts my mask on Preacher's face, all in one swift, two-handed motion. Somehow I feel that my surprised skin reaches in a great pneumatic kiss to Preacher's mask, and when this mask is in place it dissolves into my face—or rather my face seems to pour into the mold of it like hot wax, lumping into the corners the bones make. Next, the wigs. Yes. Now the crisp curls of red hair smother my skull, and, it seems, my thinking. I stare harder into the mirror to see if my metamorphosis is completed so quickly, but the mirror now shows a huge yellow desert sealed, like a pot by a lid, by a blue sky. Far away, a four-legged figure. I stare and stare, and now I can feel the form of myself runnel down my eye-beams like water in a pipe until finally I myself stand within this arid prospect. But now I am diminished; I am only three feet tall. I begin walking thirstily toward the distant figure, until at last I perceive that it is not four-legged at all; it is my grandfather standing dead still, supporting himself on his crutch and his cane. As I advance toward him, he grows taller and huger. When I finally reach him I am no taller than the ankle of his swollen foot. I shout up to him, my voice like the chirp of a desiccated flute. He answers in a voice like cannons booming. "I never did like redheaded fellers," he thunders. "They're all no-count sons of bitches." Suddenly, I am much taller, my head as high as his thigh. He pats the crisp mat of my red hair. "But you're pretty good," he says. "A feller can get around you all right. All he's got to do is just forgive. That aint as hard of a job as you would think it is. I never did understand you, though." "What do you mean?" My voice is the shattering squeak of early adolescence. "You know it too," he says. "I knew a feller like that once." "Who was that?" "I disremember his name. He was about like you, I reckon: they was somethin chinchy goin on inside of him all the time. You wouldn't of knew it unless you knew him good, though. But when he died everybody found it out. They took him to the hospital and laid him in bed and they was a little white rat gnawed its way out of his stomach. That rat had been at him all the time. Nobody knew it. That rat wasn't even as big as my hand." He throws his hand before my face. It is as big as the haunch of a horse. Suddenly in his tough palm, a rose opens and begins to bloom like the stigmata of holy men. "Everything is 'like' to you," he booms. "No, it isn't," I shout. "It's just the way they are. I know you never have understood how I couldn't. All the 'likes' kept looking at me. I had to talk about it. I never was as mean as you thought." "What?" His voice is very distant, not as if he were going away, but as if he were a ghost. "I don't know," I shout. My voice rebounds about me. I have the feeling that if I were to shout again so loudly the walls of my bedroom would fall down about me, the splinters of the pine slatting splashing up like drops of water. I sit at my black desk, writing a long epic poem about the dangers of masturbation. Looking at the blue-ruled white paper, I watch words stringing themselves out across the lines like snakes crawling along a wire fence. *This is the fat golden girl you love so much.* I lean back from the desk, and look at the walls of my room. A long red slash of grain in the shape of an arrow now changes to an arm of flame. A gray curl of smoke, and now the room is afire.

174

OR,

Here in the black woods with Uncle, the hour very close to total night, the sky blackly purple. We are squatting on our heels, hidden in the edge of a laurel thicket, looking into a dim clearing past the leaves before us. Mildly damp, dusky odor of the autumn night coming. Uncle stares, his face as locked as stone. The *reeping* of the summer's last crickets surrounds us like airy water. Leaves rubbing, branches cracking, the brush of the far side of the clearing begins to stir, mumbling after a long sleep. A flat black shape coalesces against the rather lighter surroundings. Uncle brings his rifle up. I bring mine up, the opposed hairs of my gunsight seeking the center of the dark beast, which is rather like a bear, rather like a hippopotamus. I jerk the trigger. The black beast doubles in size, a pumped balloon, and then seeps to the ground like a pool of ink, as flat now as a shadow. From this black patch up floats a shining ghost, yellow and scary in the darkness. The ghost of Judy. It expands until it fills the air above the clearing, and I suddenly jump up. I stretch my arms toward it automatically, as naturally as I would turn the palms of my hands to a campfire on a cold night. Her heavy ghost elevates perpendicularly, a slow and silent movement. It floats the air in an attitude of sleeping, clothed in the shiny cheesecloth that Sunday-school angels are always pictured in. I rush to the middle of the clearing and leap up to grasp her. I feel that I could snatch this empty ghost, crush it to a gleaming ball, and keep it forever, a nostrum, a jewel. Again and again I jump up, the bright figure only just beyond my finger tips. It floats away, higher and higher as I stare and stretch, until at last I have lost it among

175

the clouds of stars. And now the black shadows of the woods—it has become fully dark—pour around me. Like a pool they suck me down into a small cramped space: the front seat of a tiny automobile. The car is hurtling along at a terrific speed. I sit at the steering wheel unable to control or to change the movement; my hands are manacled behind my back. Landscape funnels past me, flashing in the headlights: great, tough rocks with the features of faces, the thin-fingered trees of Walt Disney cartoons, walls, water-falls, animals. Finally the car sticks, gurgles, and becomes silent. I am in a wide, but not deep, marsh. The car settles into the marsh some inches and rests. It is difficult to breathe. The headlights show only miles of shiny ground and clumps of reeds. Then the car rocks back and forth: something is shaking it. I am afraid to look behind. The shaking stops, begins again, stops. A rapping at the window. I see that it is my father. He is wearing a large mackinaw jacket and his breath streams whitely in the air. He is talking and gesticulating, but I can hardly hear his words inside the car. His voice is very small. "Turn the motor on," he says, pinching his thumb and index finger together and twisting his hand clockwise. "Turn your wheel the other way." Holding an imaginary steering wheel between his doubled hands, he heels it counter clockwise. I shout back: "My hands. I can't. My hands are tied." "Turn it to the left," he shouts. He turns his airy wheel to the left. "My hands." "Turn your motor on." He pinches the air and twists it. "My hands are tied," I shout furiously. He steps back, and holds up his right hand. "*Manus dextra*," he says, pointing to this hand with his left hand. He puts up his left hand, pointing with his right. "*Manus sinistra*." I am sweating and ex-hausted; I just shake my head. He leans forward to the

176

window to look at me closely, and his breath clouds the window until his face is only a dim pale patch. This pale patch becomes round in the plane fog, and I realize that I must have been staring at the moon for a very long time now. My hands in my pockets, I step back from the upstairs window and turn around. My grandfather and Preach sit under a naked suspended light bulb playing chess on the marble-topped table. They do not seem to notice me, bent and intent upon their game. As silently as possible, I move toward them. "Your move," says my grandfather. "Look," says Preacher, "look here." He points out a broken line of pieces on the board. "It's the Big Dipper. Look at that." I watch as he traces the shape, his finger moving in the air above the pieces. I notice that every piece on the board is a rook. "What's the use of that?" my grandfather asks. "That don't do nobody no good." He lifts his head. "I knew a feller like you one time," he says. "He was just like you, always seein somethin foolish like that." Preach asks, "What happened to him?" "He burned to death. His house burned up. When they found him, they wasn't nothin left but a black piece of wood, just the size of a walkin cane." "Well," Preacher says, "that's some use, aint it? A feller can use a good walkin cane." "Go on and move." As Preacher stretches his hand toward one of the black rooks, my grandfather slashes across his hand quickly with an opened pocketknife. One of Preacher's fingers drops solid and unbleeding on the chess board. He looks angrily at the old man. "You don't have no call to do that," he says. "What's the use of that?" "You're a no-count son of a bitch," my grandfather says. "I'm going to cut your cod out. That's about the only thing that's goin to suit me finally, I reckon." "You old hoppin Jesus," says Preach. "You've got it to do, by

177

God." "That's all right," says Jack Davis. "I can do it all right. It won't take much to do that." Jack Davis is a big Negro. He looks as if he is about eight feet tall, two hundred fifty pounds. He is wearing a red sweatshirt and bell-bottomed dungarees supported by a wide, glass-studded leather belt. His white teeth are filed and there is red paint on his lips. He is decorated for a war between rival cannibal tribes. I lie across the room on a dusty sofa. I feel very sick, almost ready to vomit. "You just better take it slow and easy now, Jack Davis," says Judy. She sits in the center of the room, rocking swiftly back and forth in a broken leather-covered rocking chair. "I know you. The way you go at it it won't be no fun at all. It won't last long enough to be a bit of fun, not a single bit. Now you just take it slow and easy." "No need for you to worry," Jack Davis says. He walks slowly across the room to me, and stands towering over me like something built precariously of toy blocks. He stretches his hand toward me and I clasp it eagerly. He pulls me steadily to my feet and pats me tenderly at the small of my back. "Are you ready now?" he asks. "Yes," I answer in a hoarse whisper. "We'd better get started then." "All right." Arm in arm we advance slowly toward Judy in her rocking chair. Her face is angry. "All right now," she says. "You know better than that. That's not what I meant at all, that's not what I was talkin about." We advance. Her face is full of fear. "By God," she cries, "you just better keep away from me." Jack Davis strikes her with his black fist. A purple patch spreads over her right cheek. "Goddamnit," she cries, "you better watch what you're doin." He hits her again and again. "Go ahead," he says to me, "go ahead." Finally I hit her, not too hard, in her soft belly. It is like putting my hand in a bowl of gelatin. I recoil

178

in disgust. But now it is too late: she sags in the middle like a half-emptied sack of flour. Dead. The room becomes brighter and brighter with sunlight. My little sister Julia stands beside me, gazing down at the still body on the cool cement floor. The sunlight shines in her yellow hair. She turns her round face up to me, a tiny tear in each eye. "It's going to be all right, isn't it?" she asks. "They say it will be all right. Isn't everything going to be all right, James?" I take her damp, chubby hand in my own dry hand. "Oh yes," I say, "it'll be all right." Now, I think, now I am a grown-up man.

OR,

I dream that I lie asleep dreaming. I stand apart watching my dreaming body on the bed, and I can feel the conspiracy tightening about me. Even so, I do not know who the conspirators are: only an urgent premonition apprises me of the plot. The idea of the plot is simple and horrible enough—merely to bar me from conscious awakening, to seal me forever in this circular dream. I press against the gate, but it does not yield; I cannot burst awake. A feeling much like that which a drowning man must have as he feels his last strength leaking away and the heavy water sucking and belching at his ears. I realize that a direct assault upon the dream itself is useless. Trench-coated, smoking a dangling cigarette, I leave my house and go into a street which I do not recognize. Standing at a corner under a streetlamp which throws a yellow light (although it is but a gray midafternoon) stands a slender girl with her back to me. She is wearing a bright silk dress. She crosses the street, and I follow her. I follow her for a couple of blocks in the quickly thickening light until she

179

turns into a large restaurant, Victorian architecture. The restaurant is filled with large round tables, linen-covered, shiny with silver and glassware. At one very large table sits the group of persons whom I recognize immediately as those who plot against me; I know them all. There sits my grandmother and grandfather, my mother and father, Uncle, Hurl, Preacher, Judy, Mavis, Jack Davis. They are all formally attired: the men tall and sinister in white tie and tails, the women suave and dark in pale evening gowns. They are all silently drunk, and although they do not speak to each other, there is much thumping at the table and banging of cutlery and glass. The girl I have followed goes into the men's room, and I sneak carefully past the table of my enemies. I am very frightened that they will notice me. But when I get into the men's room, there is no one present; the girl is not there. I search the place carefully, and, lifting the lid of the cistern of the toilet, I find a map taped there. I hear a bumping at the door and Preacher's voice saying, "He's here. I'm sure I saw him come in." I tear the map away and stuff it into my pocket. Unfastening my belt and taking off my tie, I knot them together, slip up the bathroom window, and fix my escape rope to the radiator pipe. I lower myself to the ground and run away. Glancing over my shoulder, I see a red flash of Preacher at the open window. When I feel that I have run far enough, I take out the map. There is a note at the edge of it: *This will take you there.* Shocked, I see that it is my wife's handwriting. She has even signed her name, *Sylvia.* I begin to follow the directions of the map. After coursing swiftly through many streets and alleys I find myself at what looks to be a subway entrance. I descend, but soon there is not room to stand up and the place is growing darker and darker. Then it is completely black

180

and I have to crawl on my hands and knees. A point of gray light shows ahead, but now the passage is so small that I have to wiggle forward on my belly. At last I can stand again, and I walk into a very long, very high room. It is cold here. Before me, on a long, raised slab of icy marble lies a naked giant. I think at first that he is dead, but then I notice his breathing which, in this huge cold room, is like a relentless fanning. Then I see that this sleeping giant is myself. I have come the long way about, and now my task is to arouse him. I must get him to wake. I think of the motto of the Emperor Augustus: "You got millions in you and you spend pennies. I can't make you out, boy." I pinch the cold, stonelike flesh of the huge form. I pull the flat hair on his head. Then I discover a pile of novels and magazines in one corner of the room. Pausing only to note that they are garishly colored, I tear handfuls of pages from these volumes and set fire to them. I press my improvised torch to various places on the white body. A murmuring like far thunder. The sleeping giant begins to stir. In a moment he will surge to consciousness. A dizzy blackness assails me, covering me suddenly like a dropped cloak. A flurry of realization, and I know that when this cold figure wakes I myself, a figure in his dreaming, will be forever obliterated.

These are dreams, and not nightmares. I dream my dream and swim slowly awake. The bedroom window is filled with the white light of early morning. I am not frightened or disturbed or even puzzled by my dreaming; I have watched one or more of these dreams rather as if I have been watching a train of circus animals pass on the road. The dreams speak without accusing, and they return to me night after night. In a way, I am going to school and my instructor chalks on the black-board again and again the same lessons. Even so, my attitude toward these visitations is ever more complex and more personal: they are like persons, they are like friends, without whom I would be lonely if not lost entirely; the first hint of them in my head is like the warm grasp of a familiar handshake. And yet, they awe me too, with their brightness and moral insistence. They are lightly oppressive

> *like the weight*
> *Of cathedral tunes,*

and have the same comforting force as those hymns which I have known since my childhood. They do not fever my imagination, they do not stir my fear. I lie in bed, thinking of them and watching them slowly fade away in my head like ether evaporating into the air. What shall I do? Here I lie awake a short time before the children begin to rouse and talk to each other in the adjoining bedroom. Sylvia lies lightly beside me, breathing slowly, her slender legs crossed with her right ankle on her left knee, making the number 4. Her body is turned toward the north wall, away from me. Sometimes, in this hour, I am so full of her presence that I tremble. What shall I do? I need not worry; things are going to fall into the shape that they make for themselves. The pawns will all be ranked defensively in front of the bishops, knights, and rooks. Bad, naked event will cover itself over again with my mind like an old man pulling the blankets about himself in a winter night.

I know what I shall do. I turn to Sylvia and slip my left arm beneath her left arm and put my hand desperately between her breasts. She mumbles and moves.

"You won't leave me, will you?" I whisper.

182

"Don't be silly," she mutters. She is not even awake.

"You won't, then?"

"Don't be silly. You're just being silly." She is still asleep.

I lie waiting for John and Missy to awake and for my family to rise for breakfast. The roof is dripping with the morning dew, a patient zodiac sprawls the sky.

$\mathcal{V}$OICES OF THE $\mathcal{S}$OUTH

Doris Betts, *The Astronomer and Other Stories*

Sheila Bosworth, *Almost Innocent*

Erskine Caldwell, *Poor Fool*

Fred Chappell, *The Gaudy Place*

Fred Chappell, *It Is Time, Lord*

Ellen Douglas, *A Lifetime Burning*

Ellen Douglas, *The Rock Cried Out*

George Garrett, *An Evening Performance*

George Garrett, *Do, Lord, Remember Me*

Shirley Ann Grau, *The House on Coliseum Street*

Shirley Ann Grau, *The Keepers of the House*

Barry Hannah, *The Tennis Handsome*

William Humphrey, *Home from the Hill*

Mac Hyman, *No Time For Sergeants*

Madison Jones, *A Cry of Absence*

Willie Morris, *The Last of the Southern Girls*

Louis D. Rubin, Jr., *The Golden Weather*

Evelyn Scott, *The Wave*

Lee Smith, *The Last Day the Dogbushes Bloomed*

Elizabeth Spencer, *The Salt Line*

Elizabeth Spencer, *The Voice at the Back Door*

Allen Tate, *The Fathers*

Peter Taylor, *The Widows of Thornton*

Robert Penn Warren, *Band of Angels*

Robert Penn Warren, *Brother to Dragons*

Joan Williams, *The Morning and the Evening*